Strangers and Sojourners
in a Town Called Penryn:

Adeline

by Monica Gillman Gavia

**Strangers and Sojourners
in a Town Called Penryn:**

ADELINE

Strangers and Sojourners in a Town Called Penryn:

ADELINE

Forward

Strangers and Sojourners in a Town Called Penryn: Adeline is based on a true story. It is filed under fiction because the many "holes" in the story were creatively filled in with research information and my imagination of how things might have occured. The names of the principal characters have been changed to protect the privacy of any living relatives, should there be any. It is not my intention, by relating Adeline's life story, to disparage any person, place, or institution. My only desire is to share her remarkable life story with others.

Monica Gillman Gavia
Penryn, California

**Strangers and Sojourners
in a Town Called Penryn:**

ADELINE

Strangers and Sojourners in a Town Called Penryn:

ADELINE

Prologue

Penryn, California
May 1962

I wasn't consulted about the move, didn't help pack for the move, and didn't pay much attention to the boxes that lined the hallway of our soon deserted house. The fact I can't recall such details is not too surprising; it took place more than fifty years ago, just before my eighth birthday. My brother, who was nine-and-a-half at the time, can still recall the move, the truck that hauled the household goods, and the people who helped with the move. My sister was just nine months old, so, of course, her recollection is nonexistent.

I do remember my first night at the new, old house. Dad, unable to find his tools, worked on assembling bed frames with a butter knife. Mom searched through the myriad of unmarked cardboard boxes, trying to find the sheets, pillow cases, and pillows. Being more of a hindrance instead of help in this situation, I wandered outside to inspect

Strangers and Sojourners in a Town Called Penryn:

ADELINE

the old fruit packing shed on our property that stood smack dab in the middle of a plum orchard.

    Broken wooden fruit crates were scattered about along with the thin packing papers used in lining the bottom of the crates. Shelving that once graced the walls now hung precariously, lopsided, ready to crash to the floor. There was no electrical lighting in the shed. The internal darkness illuminated only by the faint glow of the rising full moon. The shadows and images created by the moonlight gave rise to my imagination of unseen creatures and ghosts crouching in the murky corners of the building. Feeling a bit panicky, I sat on the outer ledge of the shed where I could see my mom and dad through the front room window of the house.

    The full moon brought to my mind a song and I hummed the tune for a while, then broke out into full voice. No one would hear me, no one was near as my soulful serenade to the moon sounded through the stillness of the abandoned orchard. Down the gravel road, about a mile away from where I sat, another girl, just about my age, sang her lonely tune to the full moon.

Strangers and Sojourners in a Town Called Penryn:

ADELINE

Like me, she, too, was a recent newcomer to this area. She, too, had no say so in the move. The only difference between us was that of time. For me, it was the springtime of 1962. For her, Adeline, it was the fall of 1853.

In 1962, I sat in an abandoned fruit shed, looking up at a full moon, recollecting the past few days of my family's move. In 1853, Adeline sat on a large granite mound, looking up at the very same moon, recollecting her ten month journey from Lafayette Springs, Mississippi to the the small gold-mining town of Stewart's Flat, California. Like me, she tried to sing her sorrow, but the sound that came forth from her in the emptiness of the night was an almost voiceless sob.

The move from Mississippi to California had upended Adeline's life, almost like a whirlwind had caught her up into its circulating vortex, spinning her round and round, taking her away from slave life in Mississippi, and depositing her into the foreign land of California. And all on account of the wedding of her mistress, Mary Susan Avans to Joseph Landmerac Goldstan, on January 15, 1853.

Strangers and Sojourners in a Town Called Penryn:

ADELINE

Chapter 1

Therefore do not be anxious about tomorrow, for tomorrow will be anxious for itself. Sufficient for the day is its own trouble.
Matthew 6:34

Lafayette Springs, Mississippi
January 1853

Adeline sat perched in the servants' isolated stairwell, thankful that the preparations for the wedding were almost complete. Removing her indoor shoes, she stretched her weary toes, reached down and massaged them through their coarse woolen stockings. Closing her eyes, she leaned her head against the rough-sawn pine wall, shutting out the craziness that had taken control of the Avans household.

Despite her full-time duty as a personal house servant-in-training to the upcoming bride, additional tasks and responsibilities had been heaped upon the eight-year-old slave girl. Today, after hand-washing, drying, and ironing her Mistress Mary's camisoles and petticoats, she had been summoned by Hannah, the cook, to sift a five-pound bag of

Strangers and Sojourners in a Town Called Penryn:

ADELINE

flour. Once done with the sifting, Hannah plopped a hefty portion of fresh-churned butter into a large crockery bowl, covered the creamy mound with molasses, handed the lot over to Adeline, gave her a wooden spoon, and instructed her to "beat de livin' daylights out of it!" All of these chores taxed the young girl's forearm muscles. When another older servant called to her to help clean the bedrooms, Adeline begged off, using her aching arms as an excuse. But the eight-year-old's supplications seemed to raise the older servant's hackles, earning Adeline the unpleasant task of cleansing all the bedrooms' chamber pots. Upon the swift completion of this last chore, her duties had changed once again, to that as the designated "fetcher" to whoever might call out for her.

"Adeline, go'n fetch me some eggs!"

"Adeline, carry the linens to the guests' rooms 'n make sure them beds be ready!"

"Adeline, child, hurry up! Bring me potatoes from da root cellar!"

"Adeline, come. . ."

"Adeline, find. . ."

Strangers and Sojourners in a Town Called Penryn:

ADELINE

"Adeline, gather. . .!"

Now, harried Adeline sat alone on the stairwell landing, relishing the few moments that she was able to steal for herself, away from the control of *others*. For the past six years, ever since her second birthday, her waking days, hours, minutes, movements, and tasks, were set and ordered by those *others*, without any consideration of her age and capabilities.

Those *others* determined if she would live, where she would live, who she would live with, and what type of slave she would become. Adeline didn't even remember her mother's name or recall how her mama looked. The *others* had separated mother and daughter when Adeline reached two years of age, placing her with the Avans plantation, the only place she could remember as being "home." As she pondered the familiar surroundings, a fearful unease of leaving the familiar plantation fell upon her. The gray, two-storied house was her stability. The daily routines and commands, her comfort. The sporadic personal interaction with the Avans indoor slaves, her source of affection.

Strangers and Sojourners in a Town Called Penryn:

ADELINE

She understood her place in the Avans household—to be Miss Mary's helper—for life. Understood that wherever the newlywed couple decided to reside would become Adeline's residence as well. She tried to be excited for the upcoming changes but a touch of melancholy dampened her careful optimism.

In spite of all her uncertainties, Adeline's happiness for the forthcoming wedding of Miss Mary to Mr. Joseph calmed her misgivings. Since his return to Mississippi he had not left Mary's side. The young housemaid had studied them together; how they talked and laughed, how Joseph deferred to Mary's wishes, how Mary esteemed Joseph. The years that Joseph had spent apart from Mary, searching for gold in the foothills of northern California, seemed to have strengthened the couple's affection for one another; their devotion obvious, even to a young girl like Adeline.

"Adeline, girl! Where you be? I needs more eggs!" The cry from the kitchen galley reached deep into the servants' stairwell, pulling Adeline back to her duties. Rousing from the step, she slipped the shoes back onto her tired feet, pulled up her stockings, and hollered back, "I be comin'!"

Strangers and Sojourners in a Town Called Penryn:

ADELINE

On January 15, 1853, three years after Joseph had left for California, twenty-one-year-old Mary Susan Avans and twenty-eight-year-old Joseph Landmerac Goldstan pledged "'til death us do part." Friends, family, and house slaves witnessed the exchange of promises. Solemn, inconspicuous Adeline grew teary-eyed at the spectacle of love and happiness visible on her mistress's glowing face.

The vows, repeated. The pronouncement, proclaimed. The wedding feast, commenced. Roasted hams baked with dried spiced apples, shuck beans simmered overnight with bits of bacon, tureens full of creamy corn chowder, mashed potatoes piled high—a river of butter flowing from its peaks, whipped sweet potatoes sprinkled with chopped pecans, crispy bite-sized pieces of deep-fried okra. The dancing of the wedding waltz to the couple's favorite tune. The unwrapping of the wedding presents—tinware, silverware, embroidered tablecloth and napkins, goose down pillows, a memory quilt. The cutting of the cake—a towering seven-layer yellow concoction swathed in buttercream frosting. All feats accomplished in a day's time.

Strangers and Sojourners in a Town Called Penryn:

ADELINE

Adeline marveled at the number of people who attended. "My Lordy!" she muttered. January was not the usual month for weddings in Lafayette Springs, Mississippi. Who could expect the invited to venture out in their wagons and carriages in the middle of winter when the air was so cold that it chilled a body to its very bones—when the constant rainfall turned into biting sleet that stung any exposed part of the body? Yet, most of those invited had come and lingered longer than society deemed appropriate. As Adeline busied herself tidying up the parlor, she caught snippets of the guests' conversations.

"Don't they make a beautiful couple?"

"Ben and Ollie are so proud of Mary and their new son-in-law."

"Mary waited three long years for this day. She sure looks happy. Makes me want to get married all over again!"

Adeline studied Miss Mary's face. Her mistress's married joy seemed to infuse the household. She also noted that those invited remained longer than the hosts (and servants) had anticipated.

Strangers and Sojourners in a Town Called Penryn:

ADELINE

Nobody be aleavin'...theys so happy for Miz Mary and Mr. Joseph.

Tears formed in the corners of Mary's eyes as the bride hugged each guest and well-wisher. *Miz Mary be cryin' happy tears.*

She listened as Mary explained to the well-wishers the reason for having such mixed emotions. "Yes, Joseph and I will be leaving tomorrow. I am fearfully sad to be leaving mama and papa, but, thankfully, we do not intend to stay away forever. Joseph wants me to share in his California adventure, and I am looking forward to seeing all that my husband has seen. Plus, I will have him all to myself!"

Across the parlor, a crowd of menfolk surrounded Joseph, their eagerness of learning about California gold apparent in their questions.

"Is the gold just waitin" to be picked up?"

"How did you and the Stewart boys ever come acrost the place?"

"Do you think I should give gold-mining a try?"

Strangers and Sojourners in a Town Called Penryn:

ADELINE

This last question, stated with such enthusiasm, caught the man's wife's attention. She strode across the room, grasped her husband's arm and maneuvered him away from the group of men, all the while staring long and hard at Joseph.

Adeline, tasked with refilling the buffet table, witnessed (along with many of the wedding guests) the wife wag her finger at her defeated husband, turn and point at Joseph, then whirl back around and continue shaking her finger at her husband. Adeline stifled a giggle. *I guess he won't be agoin' no wheres.*

Other utterances circulated around the room from guest to guest, all out of the hearing of the bride and groom. These whispered comments and speculations did, however, reach Adeline's ears since no one paid any mind to a common black servant girl picking up the guests' dirty dishes, or to the one replenishing an empty water glass.

"I heard they struck it rich. . .millionaires, overnight. . ."

"Don't never have to work again. . .building a mansion. . ."

Strangers and Sojourners in a Town Called Penryn:

ADELINE

"Wonder if they might spot me a stake..."

Adeline tried to understand how these people were so caught up with finding gold. *Dey has so much already...dey don't need no gold. Why dey want to go away from home?* Her attention turned to Mary and Joseph. *I jes' cain't understands why Mr. Joseph an' Miz Mary wantin' to be goin' back to Californya? Leavin' all their kinfolk behind.* She shook her head at such absurdity, and vowed, *If I ever gets me a true fam'ly, I ain't never ever gonna leab 'em. No matter how much gold there mighten be in dis whole wide world. If'n when I has a fam'ly.*

Strangers and Sojourners in a Town Called Penryn:

ADELINE

Chapter 2

*Look to the right and see:
there is none who takes notice of me;
no refuge remains to me; no one cares for my soul.
Psalm 142:4*

Adeline remained at the back of the room. She listened as the newlyweds said their good-byes, hugged their loved-ones, then said more good-byes. The difficulty of leaving their families delayed the start of Mary and Joseph's honeymoon journey by three hours. Despite the couple's scheduled timeline of a year-long honeymoon, there was the very real possibility that neither the bride nor the groom might not see their Mississippi relatives and neighbors again. Anything could happen within a year's time. Providence doesn't always line up with the plans of man. This understanding of life's vagaries dampened the newlywed's eagerness for their forthcoming wedding trip to New York City and their subsequent steamship voyage to California.

The melancholy in their many farewells awakened an ache in Adeline's heart; a distant memory of a long ago,

Strangers and Sojourners in a Town Called Penryn:

ADELINE

tearful, good-bye. *Who sayin" good-bye t' me? Why she be cryin"? When dis happen? I wisht I could 'member.*

"Adeline. . ." No answer. "Adeline. . ." Again, no answer. "Adeline!"

Called back to the present by Miss Mary's forceful voice, Adeline answered, "Yes, ma'am, I be right there." Maneuvering her way around the crowd of guests with a quiet, "scuse me, sir, ma'am", she reached the front of the well-wishers and positioned herself near Mary and awaited her mistress's inquiries and instructions.

"Adeline, is everything in place for my departure?"

"Yes, ma'am. I done checked it all myself. . . again. . .for the fifth time." This last addendum muttered under her breath.

Earlier that morning, Adeline, under harsh direction and supervision of an older personal servant, had finished packing the bride's large fashionable burnished mahogany portmanteau. After several attempts to close the overstuffed traveling box failed, Adeline hopped up on the lid. Her weightiness held the top down while her adult helper secured it shut with buckled leather straps.

Strangers and Sojourners in a Town Called Penryn:

ADELINE

Afterwards, she folded and stowed her own clothes and few earthly possessions into an unfashionable, frayed, velour, carpetbag. She, too, would be journeying west. Adeline, like every other piece of Mary's luggage and property, was being dispatched to California—to the start-up mining town of Stewart's Flat; to Mary and Joseph's honeymoon home.

When first told of the upcoming cross-country move, Adeline assumed she would be accompanying the newlywed's on their trip to New York and then venture with them onward to California. She was Mary's domestic and logic dictated that wherever the mistress went, her helper traveled with her. However, instead of traveling with the honeymooners, Mary had devised other traveling arrangements for Adeline. She foisted Adeline upon family friend William Barton and his own family's upcoming journey to California. In hindsight, Adeline recognized the early planning that Mary undertook to be free of her during the couple's voyage to California.

***

Strangers and Sojourners in a Town Called Penryn:

ADELINE

Two weeks before the wedding, Mary had suggested that William, Catheraine, and baby Annelia, arrive early at the Avans plantation. Coming from Indiana, this would allow them to rest up before the big day. She even offered Adeline as caretaker for the child, allowing the young mother, Catheraine, a chance to catch up on much needed sleep. Adeline, already over-burdened with household chores and wedding preparation chores, dreaded this new time-intensive task. But instead of being a burden, this added assignment became a treat for Adeline. She relished every moment spent with the baby. She watched the babe while the mother rested and Joseph and William conferred. All morning. All afternoon. All evening.

Adeline wondered how they could talk so much. *What dey talks about so much? Lordy, dey do talk.* She took pains to be nearby the two men, just so her curiosity might be satisfied. She gleaned from the discussions that William and Catheraine also planned to leave their home state, Indiana, for the great state of California, traveling cross county by wagon train.

Strangers and Sojourners in a Town Called Penryn:

ADELINE

During one such conversation, Adeline overheard Miss Mary off-handedly suggest to William that while on the long trek to California, Catheraine might benefit by having a helper.

William mulled over the proposal. "Who did you have in mind, Mary? I know that Catheraine could use a little extra help in keeping baby 'Lia in tow." He looked across the parlor to his child, to see that the toddler had, once again, escaped from his wife's hold. Adeline, being nearest to the wandering babe, guided the tot back to her mother. William watched his daughter smile and giggle at the young slave girl and pretended to come to Adeline, a diversionary tactic. The toddler scurried past Adeline. Surprised at the baby's evasion, Adeline laughed aloud and chased after the mischievous girl.

William grinned at his daughter's resourcefulness then returned his attention back to Mary. "As you can see, Mary, 'Lia is quite the handful. Now, who do you have in mind?"

Strangers and Sojourners in a Town Called Penryn:

ADELINE

Mary turned her head towards the young slave and nodded, indicating to William her choice of who should accompany them on their westward journey.

Out of the corner of her eye, Adeline saw Mary's gesture. Unsure of what it meant, but sensing that they were discussing her, Adeline's heart rate doubled. On the pretense of guiding baby 'Lia around the room, Adeline drew nearer to William and Mary. Now within hearing range, she gave full attention to their dialog.

Mary continued. "Well, I was just thinking that since Joseph and I will be on our honeymoon voyage to California, maybe Adeline could accompany your family. She would be of great help to Catheraine and the baby, and it would give Joseph and I some privacy during our journey."

William paused, looked at Adeline, then responded, his words chosen with care. "I think that would work out just fine for us, Mary. Although I don't adhere to the tenets of slavery, we will take Adeline along with us as our guest and helper. As a matter of fact, we will take her back with

Strangers and Sojourners in a Town Called Penryn:

ADELINE

us to Indiana when we leave here. She can become accustomed to our ways before we all depart for California."

They both turned their attention, once again, to Adeline, who now held the squirming 'Lia on her knee. Adeline looked up to see William and Mary staring at her. She lowered her eyes then glanced up again. William continued gazing at her, a quizzical look in his eye, while Mary paid no more attention to her than she would to an ordinary housefly, just another bother in life.

Turmoil and tumult arose within Adeline. She looked around the parlor, the dining room, the sitting room. To everything that was familiar to her. *I soon be leavin' dis place. I be leavin' all I ever knowed and travlin' with strangers to a strange town.* She looked, again, at William. He was still watching her. He nodded at Adeline. Eyes lowered, she nodded back, somehow calmed by this acknowledgment.

Later on that evening, in the privacy of an upstairs sitting room, Mary dictated to Adeline what her transitory responsibilities on the California Trail would be.

Strangers and Sojourners in a Town Called Penryn:

ADELINE

"Adeline, you will take care of one-year-old Annelia Elizabeth Barton while traveling. This will give relief to Catheraine and also help prepare you for the skills needed to care for the children that Joseph and I will one day have. You will also do whatever-else is asked of you. Just because you are away from me does not mean that you can do as you please. And see to it that you are not bothersome to William and Catheraine."

Mary, muttering more to herself than Adeline, added, "Thankfully, this assignment will keep you out of my way and from under my feet until I have need of you again at Stewart's Flat."

Adeline simply replied. "Yes'm. I be no bother to no ones."

Strangers and Sojourners in a Town Called Penryn:

ADELINE

Chapter 3

*I lie awake; I am like a lonely sparrow
on the housetop.
Psalm 102:7*

Since that night, after learning of her fate, Adeline's apprehensions increased with each passing day. Now, after the celebration, as the newlyweds prepared to leave, the uncertainties of her upcoming journey with an unknown family to the unfamiliar world of Indiana and eventually to California caused her to cling to her departing mistress. Mary shook her off, glaring at the child. "What's got into you, Adeline? I declare." Adeline backed away, taking one last look at Miss Mary and Joseph as they ascended into the carriage.

The couple shouted their final good-byes and began their way to New York. Adeline drug her feet as she made her way down the servants' stairwell that led to the kitchen. The cook, indoor slaves, and even some of the field slaves stood around the massive work table.

Strangers and Sojourners in a Town Called Penryn:

ADELINE

"Come here girlie." Hannah, the matronly overseer of the house slaves and somewhat surrogate mother to Adeline beckoned the young slave girl into the crowded kitchen. "We wants to say our good-byes, too."

Adeline bowed her head slightly and shuffled into the room. The smell of cinnamon, nutmeg and molasses enveloped her as she drew near to Hannah. Lifting her chin just a little, she saw an apple cake placed in the middle of the table. Looking up at Hannah she whispered, "Apple be my favrit. You think I might haf a little bit 'fore I leave?"

Hannah scooped up the submissive child. "That cake be for you 'n you can haf it *all* if you wants!" All at once, everyone began talking. Words and wishes and farewells swirled around her.

"Adeline, you be soooo blest."

"Addie, wish I could be you."

"Adeline girl, tell Miz Mary that you want me to go with."

"Adeline honey, we sure be missing you, but you be favored goin' to California."

Strangers and Sojourners in a Town Called Penryn:

ADELINE

Mary and Joseph's good-byes had been sad and tearful. In contrast, the slaves' farewells, voiced all around Adeline, were cheerful, good-humored, almost festive. Why was everyone so happy for her? To eight-year-old Adeline, there was nothing joyous about the leaving. Goodbye meant parting from all she had ever known. The well-wishes of the other slaves did not bring her encouragement but rather a blanket of uneasiness that did not bring comfort.

I wants to stay here, not to go to Calfornya. I wants to be wif my slave fam'ly.

Tears filled Adeline's eyes. She lowered her head and covered her mouth with her hand, muffling her words. "I. . .I. . .I ain't wants to be goin'. I wants to stay."

But Hannah heard Adeline's restrained confession. She bent down and whispered into Adeline's ear. "California be a free state, honey. Ain't ever forgit. If you still be in California when you be growed, you ain't haf to be no one's slave!" The child nodded as if understanding what she had been told, too timid to ask what a "free state" meant. Hannah drew Adeline to her breast and enveloped her with lov-

Strangers and Sojourners in a Town Called Penryn:

ADELINE

ing arms. "I be praying for you on your journey to a new life. You 'member that. I be prayin' ev'ry day."

The servants formed a circle around Hannah and Adeline and began singing a solemn but comforting hymn to the distraught eight-year-old girl.

In da mornin, when I rise
In da mornin, when I rise
In da mornin, when I rise
Gib me Jesus.

    Gib me Jesus, gib me Jesus
    You can haf all dis world, but
    Gib me Jesus

'Twixt da cradle 'n da grave
'Twixt da cradle 'n da grave
'Twixt da cradle 'n da grave
Gib me Jesus

    Gib me Jesus, gib me Jesus
    You can haf all dis world, but
    Gib me Jesus

When I be far from home
When I be far from home

Strangers and Sojourners
in a Town Called Penryn:

ADELINE

When I be far from home
Gib me Jesus...

Adeline looked at each of the singers, memorizing their faces, determined to remember those who would not be in her life for at least a year. Slipping away from the center of the ring, she went around the circle, hugging each one, gaining the strength needed to begin her pilgrimage to California.

The Goldstan family--Mary and Joseph; the Barton family--William, Catheraine, and Annelia; and eight-year-old Adeline—three sets of travelers: two voluntary—one conscripted.

Strangers and Sojourners in a Town Called Penryn:

ADELINE

Chapter 4

Gracious words are like a honeycomb, sweetness to the soul and health to the body.
Proverbs 16:24

William Barton Residence
Mt. Vernon, Indiana
April 1853

Adeline had only been with the Barton family for two-and-a-half months, but during that time she learned how to bathe the baby 'Lia, prepare her food, feed her, dress her, and change her soiled diapers. Other tasks included the washing, drying, and folding of the baby's clothes, bedding, and, of course, undergarments. Scouring, scrubbing, and sterilizing baby bottles required a good amount of time, also. But the most important and agreeable task for Adeline to fulfill each day was the watching over and the entertaining of the year-old toddler.

At first, the daily (and nightly) routine of caring for a young toddler overwhelmed Adeline. But as the days passed, the tasks became easier and, surprisingly, enjoy-

Strangers and Sojourners in a Town Called Penryn:

ADELINE

able. She looked forward to each new day, anticipating what sweet 'Lia would learn to do next.

Miss Catheraine, pleased with Adeline's progress, commented, "I trust you with my child, Adeline. She adores you and I can tell that you care for her. Thank you for coming to help me on this trip."

Don't she know I was sent here by Miz Mary? I had no say so? Adeline looked straight at Catheraine, trying to understand her words of praise. . .for doing what she had been told to do.

"Um, thank you for taking me, ma'am." Catheraine's kindness lifted Adeline's spirits and soothed her lonesomeness. She thrived in this new, welcoming environment with its security and protectiveness. As the time came for the journey west, a more confident Adeline actually looked forward to the adventure and the time she would be spending with the Barton family.

Today. Leavin' day. Adeline stood aside of the fray, mesmerized by the Barton men scurrying back and forth between the house and the wagons, carrying baggage and

Strangers and Sojourners in a Town Called Penryn:

ADELINE

boxes, bumping into each other in the comings in and goings out, laughing and carrying on so much that all the neighbors had gathered in the dusty street to watch the family in action. What a commotion! Adeline remained far from the activity but close enough to smile at the goings on and, at the same time, keep 'Lia in tow. Eventually, some of the onlookers joined in the mayhem of the moment, shouldering the supplies, putting them in the newly made Barton Wagon Works wagon. William had personally designed and built his home on wheels, one of the last wagons to be built at the Barton family blacksmith/wagon shop. Much thought went into the construction, from the many nooks, cupboards, and storage bins, to the foldaway bed slats that served as inside sitting benches during the day.

William directed where the provisions were to be stowed while the womenfolk supervised and womanly, but sternly, barked out their concerns.

"Be careful with that box! The family china is in there!"

"Can't you make room for Catheraine's settee?"

Strangers and Sojourners in a Town Called Penryn:

ADELINE

"Maybe you should put that basket up in front of the wagon and move that other box to the back."

Adeline sensed their good intentions—but their attempts to be a help during this time of departure only slowed down (intentionally?) the process, hampering William and Catheraine's departure for California. Futile. Just as Adeline's passionate petition to remain at the plantation had been futile.

The Barton women, realizing the permanence of the situation, that William, Catheraine and 'Lia would not be present at any future family gatherings, remained by the wagon, their quiet goodbyes growing louder, interspersed with a sniffle, a hanky lifted to the eyes, then all out sobs.

"I. . . will. . . . . write. . . ev'ry week," Catheraine's mother promised, "just as soon as. . .as soon as. . .you have an address."

Catheraine hugged her mother. "I'll try to send you p-p-p-postings. . .as we travel."

William interrupted the women with a gruff, "Enough, now. Hurry up your good-byeing or we will miss

Strangers and Sojourners
in a Town Called Penryn:

ADELINE

meeting up with the wagon train in St. Joseph. I don't want to be the last wagon in line, eating everyone's trail dust the whole trip." The audible sounds of crying ceased but tears still flowed. Adeline watched the women as they disentangled their hugs.

A vital part of the Barton family from Indiana was covered-wagon bound for the godless wilderness of California. It was the beginning of May, 1853, and it was time to go.

Strangers and Sojourners in a Town Called Penryn:

ADELINE

Chapter 5

*Let me hear in the morning of your steadfast love,
for in you I trust.
Make me know the way I should go,
for to you I lift up my soul.
Psalm 143:8*

**On the California Trail
May--October, 1853**

Adeline awoke early. She had learned to go to sleep fully clothed so as to get a jump star in the morning. She pulled on her supple suede boots—an unheard of, totally unexpected, but welcomed present from Miss Catheraine. After rolling up her coarse, twill, linsey-woolsey sleeping blanket and stowing it under the driving seat of the covered wagon, she set about preparing the campfire for the morning's breakfast. She wanted to sing out loud but didn't. Instead, a soft hum satisfied the urge. Singing would come later, after the dawn, after the sleeping wagon train inhabitants came to life.

Strangers and Sojourners
in a Town Called Penryn:

ADELINE

She rekindled last night embers, slowly adding small logs to the flames, creating a larger fire. Once all the logs were burning steadily, she spread them out so that they could become coals that would give off a more controlled, steady heat. While waiting for the fire to burn down, she gathered the ingredients for corn meal mush and filled a pot with water. With a fire poker, Adeline spread out the now ready embers, placed the cast iron pot of water on top of them, along with a three-legged cast iron skillet, called a spider. As the skillet became hot, she carefully added thick, slab-cut bacon slices. The bacon immediately sizzled as it hit the pan, releasing a wake-up aroma to the still-sleeping Catheraine and 'Lia. Adeline next added the currants, cornmeal, lard, and salt to the now boiling water, stirring the mixture constantly until just the right thickness. She finished frying the bacon and removed the skillet from the fire. She ladled the thick steaming cornmeal mush into four bowls, topping the hot cereal with wagon-trail-churned butter, fresh milk, and dark molasses. As the last drop of molasses plopped into the fourth bowl, Adeline spied William coming in from rounding up the cattle. Out of the corner of

Strangers and Sojourners in a Town Called Penryn:

ADELINE

her eye she spotted Catheraine, holding 'Lia, climb out of the back of the wagon. Adeline scurried over to help with the baby.

"Good mornin', Miss Cathy, Mr. William. Breakfast be ready." The family sat around the fire. William led them in their daily breakfast prayer.

After the prayer, Adeline stepped up to Catheraine, arms extended. "Let me take little Missy whiles you eat." The still sleepy child softly nuzzled Adeline's neck, causing the once timid Adeline to smile as well as giggle. Three months traveling on the California Trail with the Bartons had changed her from a solemn, obedient servant to a cheerful and willing helper.

Catheraine, done with breakfast, said, "Here, Adeline, give Missy to me. I'm finished eating. Go ahead and eat while I change and dress the baby. I'll finish feeding her as well. Thank you for such a good meal. It should carry us over until supper." The baby changed caretakers once again.

Adeline sat down beside Mr. William, balancing a plate of crisp bacon on her lap while cupping a bowl of

Strangers and Sojourners
in a Town Called Penryn:

ADELINE

warm mush with her small hand. *They treat me. . .diff'rent. Diff'rent from the Avanss. Maybe they don't know nuthin' bout servants' jobs and place. Maybe so, but I won't be tellin' 'em hows it 'spose to be.* Emboldened by the kindness and friendliness of the Bartons, she spoke hesitantly, carefully choosing her words.

"Mr. William?"

"Yes, Adeline?"

"Mr. William, I don't mean to be pert, but . . ."

"Go on Adeline."

"Well, . . .why you leavin' all the rest of your fam'ly, just to look for gold? Fam'ly be special. Gold just be, well, gold. A thing. You can find more gold, but, fam'ly? Onct they be gone, it sure be hard to find agin."

Silence. Adeline fidgeted, looking out of the corner of her eyes toward the still silent Mr. William seated beside her.

"Sometimes, Addie. . ." William paused, took a deep breath, then continued. "Sometimes, choices have to be made. Difficult choices. I had no intention of moving to California, especially to look for gold. My decision to leave

Strangers and Sojourners in a Town Called Penryn:

ADELINE

Indiana was not an easy one to make, but circumstances changed my plans. Moving merely to find gold was never my primary intention. Going to California is for Catheraine's benefit."

A longer pause. Much longer. Then William spoke a bit angrily, hurrying to get the words out, "Regardless if Catheraine agrees with me or not." He abruptly stood up, spilling his eating utensils on the ground, and walked away.

His last statement was not directed to Adeline. Rather, he had spoken to the vast western plain that lay stretched out before the wagon train—silently guiding them all to a new, undetermined life in the little town of Stewart's Flat.

* * *

The trail stretched on. Adeline's numerous daily routines kept her happily occupied from sun-up to sun-down. At times, while doing her chores, she would watch the other children as they skipped ahead of the wagons or headed off on a side trail to explore a bluff. During campfire time she caught bits and pieces of their conversations about their

Strangers and Sojourners in a Town Called Penryn:

ADELINE

daily adventures. Today's adventures were being related as the grown-ups listened half-heartedly.

"I could see all the way to the other side of the prairie, where the big mountains begin. They had snow on 'em!"

"I saw where someone had carved their name on the rock cliff's wall. 'John Stengal, age nine.'"

One young boy, not to be outdone, declared, "Well, that ain't nothin'. I seen an Indian!!!"

This last boast not only caught Adeline's attention but also the adults who heard it. William. Barton, along with the other men of the company, approached the youngster. "What's that you say, son? Don't you be telling no stories! Did you see an Indian today?"

"Well, umm, well, uh, it could've been one. It was sorta far off from where I was standing." The boy shuffled his feet a little, scratched behind his right ear and his left ear, looked askance at the glowering William Barton, then bowed his head. "Nah, if truth be told, I think it was just a little ol' rock tower."

Strangers and Sojourners in a Town Called Penryn:

ADELINE

Adeline lifted her hand to her mouth, stifling back a laugh as the men lectured the boy on the consequences of telling lies.

Indians, huh, I wisht I could see one, just to say I seen one. She finished up her evening chores, unrolled her blankets under the wagon, contentedly laid down, and whispered, "Dear Lord Jesus, maybe you can let me see an Indian 'fore we get to California, okay? Oh, an' make sure he be a real friendly one. Amen."

***

Every first Sunday of the month was a day of rest for the wagon company. Well, more rest than usual. Although there was no traveling, menfolk mended the wagons, womenfolk mended the clothing, and the designated preacher mended the souls. The men of the camp took turns officiating. This Sunday was William's turn.

All of the sojourners of the wagon train attended the Sunday meeting. Some for the fellowship, some for the singing, and some for the potluck that came after the service. Adeline came to services out of her devotion to the

Strangers and Sojourners in a Town Called Penryn:

ADELINE

Bartons. She wanted to be included in whatever her temporary family did.

Sitting at the back of the group, Adeline fidgeted nervously. She smoothed out the wrinkles in her brown checkered dress, tucked an errant loop of twisted hair back under her bonnet, placed her hands in her lap, and anxiously waited to hear what her "Mr. William" had to say.

One day, about a week ago, she had confided to Catheraine that Mr. William was the

"bestest 'n kindest overseer" she had ever known. "He be almost as holy as Jesus!"

Miss Catheraine corrected her, saying, "Mr. William is not your overseer and he is certainly no saint. He is just and ordinary person like everyone else." But Adeline would have none of it. Her devotion to him had taken root slowly, blossoming each day on the journey. Now, he was firmly planted in her young, impressionable soul, her very being, and nothing could dissuade her from thinking any less of him.

"He be sent from heaven to show me how a real family should be. Of course, Miss Catheraine, you be special,

Strangers and Sojourners
in a Town Called Penryn:

ADELINE

too. But Mr. William, he be sump'um extra special." No amount of persuasion could convince her otherwise.

The Sunday service commenced. As the appointed song leader began directing the congregation in the first hymn, Adeline closed her eyes, tilted her head slightly to the right, and listened to the tune being sung. *It sure ain't like the music I know'd, but it still be purdy to my heart.* As the second verse began, Adeline hummed the melody. By the third verse, she had learned the refrain and joined in with the impromptu choral group. By the fifth verse, her voice soared through the air, rising above the others. "Amazing love! How can it be, that thou, my God, shouldst die for me? Ahh—men."

William stepped to the front of the group and removed his hat. The men in the make-shift pews followed suit.

"Let us pray. Dear Father in heaven, we thank you for your diligence in keeping watch over our long journey. We thank you for the blessings of fair weather, plentiful grasslands, and fresh water that you have provided. We pray that as we continue to our new land we will always give thanks

Strangers and Sojourners in a Town Called Penryn:

ADELINE

in remembrance of Your great goodness and mercy towards us. Amen." The congregation answered back a resounding "AMEN!".

William looked out over the assembly, acknowledging each family group with a nod. His eye lingered a little longer on Catheraine and Adeline. A smile came to his lips.

"Today, let us consider Ecclesiastes 3:1-8. This passage is a familiar one, but I want us to examine each verse a little closer.

Verse one states, '*To every thing there is a season, and a time to every purpose under the heaven;*' We are currently in a season—a season of transition, and, for some, perhaps, a season of apprehension. Many of you are wondering, 'What will happen in the future? Have I made the right decision?' Let us purpose to be in tune with God's season, with what He has in store for us at this moment in time.

'*A time to be born, and a time to die; a time to plant, and a time to pluck up that which is planted;*' Verse two reminds us that there is a pattern to our existence. We are born. And we will die. It is the same for all types of life. We cannot change what is predestined for us. We will die. But

Strangers and Sojourners in a Town Called Penryn:

ADELINE

during the time that we are alive, how shall we live? How will we respond to the trials and triumphs of life?

'A time to kill, and a time to heal; a time to break down, and a time to build up;' We must remember that when there is loss, when there is a death, when there is a dismantling of what we have built, there will come a time of healing, of rebuilding, of a new life to carry on the purpose of those that have departed.

'A time to weep, and a time to laugh; a time to mourn, and a time to dance;' We are not strangers to sadness and tears. Leaving the certainty of an established home to venture to an uncertain land caused many a tear to be shed. Yet, there will come new times of laughter and times of dancing. We have already shared many a laugh together on our journey, some even laughing while crying, and I am sure that there will be many more occasions to weep. . .and to dance.

'A time to cast away stones, and a time to gather stones together; a time to embrace, and a time to refrain from embracing;' We have cast away the stones of frivolous luxuries and gathered the stones of essentials. We have em-

Strangers and Sojourners in a Town Called Penryn:

ADELINE

braced one another on this journey, while leaving behind the embraces of our friends and families.

'A time to get, and a time to lose; a time to keep, and a time to cast away;' We have acquired new friendships while leaving behind old ones. We have kept the good memories, but cast away the ones that cause grief, laying aside any hindrance that may keep us from our destination.

'A time to rend, and a time to sew; a time to keep silence, and a time to speak;' This wilderness with its thorns and prickly bushes has torn our clothing, but not beyond mending. We have wrenched the hearts of those left behind, but by writing letters of encouragement to them, those broken hearts can be mended.

'A time to love, and a time to hate; a time of war, and a time of peace.' We have loved. We have hated. Sadly, I feel that there is a hatred rising up in this nation that may lead us to a time of war. We can only pray for God's mercy and guidance in this matter. Where there is hatred, love cannot dwell. We must pray that this country learns to love. . .everyone. We must pray for peace. . .for everyone. Our lives are in God's hands, and in His time He will make all

Strangers and Sojourners in a Town Called Penryn:

ADELINE

things beautiful. We must trust and adhere to what God has spoken. '*To every thing there is a season, and a time to every purpose under the heaven.*'

"Please, join hands with those next to you and bow your heads for the closing prayer." Catheraine took ahold of Adeline's small hand, the child's dark chestnut colored skin in sharp contrast to Catheraine's opaque whiteness. Adeline reached for the hand of the person that stood on the other side of her, but her innocent attempt was rebuffed. *"A time to love; and a time to hate."*

The regular schedule for the wagon train was to travel seven days a week with a full day of rest on the first Sunday of the month. However, sporadic breaks from traveling were taken when needed. If grassland was abundant, the group would rest and allow the oxen, horses, and cows to graze. The men would harvest the tall, thick grass with a sickle, gathering a supply for the time when no grassland would be found. Adeline called these times "lazy days" even though daily chores still needed to be done. She ea-

**Strangers and Sojourners
in a Town Called Penryn:**

ADELINE

gerly tackled her duties, one by one, anxious for some free time to explore the prairie hills and dales.

"Miss Catheraine, I done finished my early chores. I'd likes to take 'Lia for a walk."

"That is a good idea, Addie. Give me a minute and I'll join you. Don't forget to put on your bonnet."

While Catheraine prepared herself and 'Lia, Adeline sorted through her faded satchel and pulled out her head covering. She tugged at the drawstrings of her bonnet, forming an awkward bow then walked to the back of the wagon. Catheraine handed 'Lia down to her. "I'm afraid she's getting quite heavy. All this traveling seems to agree with her."

"Yes, ma'am. She be growin' plenty since Indiana. Look how she be squirmin' to git down an' walk! Do you need my help in gittin' out of the wagon?"

"Thank you Addie, but I think I can manage. I'll be glad when I can stretch out and sleep in a regular bed. I just can't seem to get enough rest."

"Maybe you might'n want to stay behind and take a nap. Might'n be better for you."

Strangers and Sojourners in a Town Called Penryn:

ADELINE

"No. I want to walk with my baby girl while I am up to it."

They each clasped one of 'Lia's hands. She looked first to her mama and then to Adeline. Her locks of golden red hair swirled from one shoulder to the other as she swung her head back and forth.

"I sure loves Missy's hair. Wisht mine were soft as hers."

"Oh, Adeline, I think your hair is beautiful. Hasn't it been easier to keep since I started brushing it for you?"

"Yes, ma'am. But it will never be as purdy as 'Lia's. Mine be too curly and plain—almost as if God ran out of colors for a darkie's hair."

"Well, I think God chose the best for you. No one else has hair the color of fresh-brewed coffee. And when it is not braided it surrounds your head and face almost like a halo." With a twinkling wink of her eye to Adeline, Catheraine continued on. "And only angels have halos, you know. God made you an angel and then sent you to our family for a time."

Strangers and Sojourners in a Town Called Penryn:

ADELINE

Silence. Adeline shyly glanced over at Catheraine, her allegiance and admiration for her friend and temporary mistress now as strong as her devotion for Mr. William. *I love you Miss Catheraine; I love you with my whole heart. I will love you as long as I live.*

Adeline's thoughts were interrupted by the sound of galloping horses. The clip-clopping of the hooves grew louder. Unaware of how much ground they had covered, Catheraine and Adeline now saw that they had wandered to the other side of a small hill and into a valley where they were not visible to the rest of the wagon train. Adeline gasped involuntarily. The horses' riders were Indians.

"Adeline, come near to me." Catheraine gathered 'Lia and Adeline, one on each side of her.

There were three Indians. . .but, thankfully to Adeline, they were women. *What harm would women Indians want to do to us, seeing as we ain't got no guns?*

They dismounted and began walking straight towards the frightened trio. Catherine picked up 'Lia and tightly held on to her child. The younger looking of the three natives boldly approached Catheraine and pointed at 'Lia,

Strangers and Sojourners in a Town Called Penryn:

ADELINE

pantomiming her desire to hold the fair-skinned baby. Catheraine drew back from the woman and clutched at 'Lia so fiercely that the toddler began to fuss. The oldest-looking Indian woman reached out and touched 'Lia's golden hair, felt her soft face, pulled on her summer dress. She took measure of 'Lia's dainty bare feet, resting them in her rough and calloused hands.

Adeline held her breath. Squeezing her eyes tightly shut, she whispered, "Dear sweet Jesus, I seen enough Indians, thank you." When she opened her eyes, she saw the Indian women jumping back onto their horses. With a wisp of dust, they were gone, galloping back to wherever they had come.

Calmly, quietly, Catheraine turned to Adeline. "Well, I think that we have had enough adventure for one day, Addy. Let's go back to camp."

The campfire story that night belonged exclusively to Adeline.

***

Three days later, Indians were sighted following the wagon train. They kept their distance but continued to ac-

Strangers and Sojourners in a Town Called Penryn:

ADELINE

company the group from afar. When the train settled down for the night, the Indians rode up to the company. Adeline watched as they approached. Her eyes grew wide. She ran to the Barton wagon. "Miss Catheraine, Miss Catheraine! They be the same Indians that we seen!"

Catheraine looked out the back of the wagon. The men of the camp had gathered round the Indian women but the native riders made no attempt to dismount. Rather, they slowly walked their horses from one wagon to another as the wagon train men followed closely behind them. Finally, the older Indian woman spotted Adeline standing alongside the Barton wagon. Catheraine sat inside, holding 'Lia.

The tribal women trotted their horses up to Catheraine, stopped, smiled, and handed her a small pair of beaded and fringed deer-skinned moccasins. Catheraine nodded to the Indian woman, acknowledging the gift. She then placed them on 'Lia. A perfect fit. Catheraine nodded again. The older Indian woman nodded back. Then the three riders once again turned their horses towards the hills and rode away.

**Strangers and Sojourners
in a Town Called Penryn:**

ADELINE

They were the first Indians that Adeline had ever seen and she prayed right then and there that they would be her last.

Strangers and Sojourners in a Town Called Penryn:

ADELINE

Chapter 6

*For I know the plans I have for you, declares the Lord,
plans for welfare and not for evil,
to give you a future and a hope.
Jeremiah 29:11*

**Hangtown, (Placerville), California
October 1853**

The long journey was almost at an end. The wagon company pulled into Hangtown, California in mid October. By William's calculations it was now only a two day ride to Stewart's Flat. To Adeline, each mile closer to their destination meant separation from this family that she had grown to love and, by all their signs of affection, had grown to love her as well.

Maybe Miss Mary 'n Mr. Joseph don't need me no mores. Maybe I can stay with Mr. William and Miss Catheraine. To Adeline, the turning of the wagon wheels, the plodding of the oxen team, the swishing of the butter bucket seemed to keep rhythm with her thoughts.

Strangers and Sojourners in a Town Called Penryn:

ADELINE

Maybe. . .maybe. . .maybe. This be the last part of the journey. I gots to talk to Mr. William beforewe gets to Stewart's Flat.

Adeline climbed from the wagon bed into the driver's seat of the wagon and sat besideWilliam. "We be almost there, Mr. William?"

"Two more days, Adeline. Then we'll be at our new home. It's a new beginning, a new life."

"Mr. William. . ." Adeline hesitated, not sure of what to say. "Mr. William, you think that Miss Mary might'n not need me anymore?"

William reassured her. "Adeline, don't worry about that. She wanted you to be with her in California. She'll be needing you for a long time."

"Well. . .maybe I don't means that she won't need me, but. . .but, well, it's just that. . .well, she don't treat me as a. . .as a. . .as a part of the fam'ly, like you 'n Miss Catheraine do. To Miss Mary, I be jes' a nes'sary bother." These last few words were spoken between sobs and tears. Trying to regain her composure, Adeline turned her face away from Mr. William. Bringing up the bottom of her

Strangers and Sojourners in a Town Called Penryn:

ADELINE

dress apron, she dabbed at the tears on her cheek then covered her eyes with the hem of the cloth and sobbed, the outward movement of her shoulders the only visible sign of her soul's inward distress.

William, still driving the wagon, encircled Adeline's shoulder with his free arm. Adeline looked up at him and noticed the tears forming at the corner of his eyes.

"Addie, I know that you want to stay with us. I hope you know that we love you as much as we love our little girl. You have become such a part of our family that it will be hard to have you leave us, but I cannot demand that Mary allow you to stay with us."

Adeline's silent sobs subsided. "I knows it. I guess Miss Mary needs me." *But she don't love me.* Adeline looked up at William. Through red-rimmed eyes she stared long and hard at the person who cared for her, no matter her skin color or station in life. The one person she could trust and rely on when others might fail her.

He continued, an earnestness in his voice. "If there comes a time when you are no longer needed at the Gold-

Strangers and Sojourners in a Town Called Penryn:

ADELINE

stan house, you will always be welcomed at mine. . .no matter what the circumstances may be. Remember that."

Comforted by his invitation, Adeline's spirits lifted. "Yessir, Mr. William. I will 'member."

***

The last leg of the journey from Hangtown to Stewart's Flat seemed to be conducted at a rapid pace. The established trail was easy traveling for the oxen and they plodded steadily along without any needed encouragement. William handed over the reins to Adeline, the last part of her overland training coming to an end. She wanted to hold the team back, to keep them from reaching their destination—her destination, yet they automatically plodded on.

P-lop, p-lop, p-lop, p-lop. *Slow down. Take your time. Slow down. Take your time.* Adeline silently willed the oxen to hold back, her inward chanting keeping time with the beasts' movements. *Not so fast, not so fast.*

"Mr. William, am I to go wif Miss Mary and Mr. Joseph tonight?"

"Yes, Addie."

Strangers and Sojourners in a Town Called Penryn:

ADELINE

"Mr. William, do you think that I might'n visit you ev'ry now 'n then?"

William thought about this for a bit. "Well, I will ask Joseph and Mary. Maybe if I suggest to them that Catheraine needs help until she gets her strength back they might see their way to let you come one day a week. That is, if Mary can do without you for a day."

"Thank you, Mr. William." *One day a week. One day a week.* Ker-plop, ker-plop, ker- plop. An audible sigh escaped from her lips, releasing her heaviness, leaving a hopeful smile behind.

Nightfall descended. The oxen clumped on. The gentle rhythm of their gait lulling Catheraine and Annelia to sleep in the lilting wagon bed.

"Mr. William, looks like someone be comin' at us." Adeline guided the oxen to the side of the trail.

Over the crest of a small hill, a large black horse cantered towards the wagon. As it drew nearer, its rider took off his hat and started waving it overhead. William and Adeline could hear him yelling, "Welcome! Welcome to Stewart's Flat! Welcome to your new home!" Adeline rec-

Strangers and Sojourners
in a Town Called Penryn:

ADELINE

ognized him first. "Why, it's Mister Joseph! I ain't never seen him so spirited!"

William plucked the reins from Adeline, abruptly stopped the wagon, jumped off the driver's seat, and ran to meet Joseph on the trail. At the same time, Joseph dismounted and ran towards William.

Adeline watched as the two men embraced, patted each other on the back, then embraced again. They talked for a bit. Adeline tried to hear what was being said but was out of listening range. She noticed that both men were looking towards her. Joseph shook his head as if in disagreement. They both looked back towards the wagon. William pointed at her then pointed at Joseph. Joseph stared at Adeline for a long while. He finally turned back to William and held out his hand. William grasped it, slowly enclosing it with his other hand. They embraced yet again. William walked back to the wagon as Joseph mounted his horse. He signaled for William to follow his lead and William urged the ox team onward.

Strangers and Sojourners in a Town Called Penryn:

ADELINE

Taking Adeline's small, quivering hand, William signed as he spoke. "Well, Adeline, let's see what Stewart's Flat holds for us."

Catheraine and 'Lia slept so soundly through the last part of the journey that they didn't wake when the wagon stopped at Joseph and Mary's house. William gathered Adeline's traveling bag and placed it on the backdoor bedroom stoop. Adeline slowly backed out of the wagon, placing her left foot on the wheel hub while reaching for the ground with her right. She remained by the wagon, unwilling to move towards the house. Finally, with bowed head, she walked reluctantly to the back of the wagon where the now awake Catheraine sat, cradling her still sleeping toddler. The exhausted mother motioned for Adeline to come closer to her. As Adeline neared, Catheraine extended her hand and touched the young girl's face. Adeline willed her tears to stay away but one escaped and fell to her cheek. Catheraine gently brushed it away. Adeline grasped Catheraine's trembling hand and marveled that a white woman and her husband had come to care for her, a com-

Strangers and Sojourners in a Town Called Penryn:

ADELINE

mon Mississippi house slave, as much as they cared for their own child.

William gave her a hug, kissed her cheek, then bent down to be at eye level with her. "Adeline, you will be visiting with us this Sunday, and every Sunday thereafter. Joseph has promised me that as long as all is calm in the Goldstan household, Sunday will be your own personal day."

He knelt down to embrace his adopted daughter once more. As he did, he whispered, "You will always be a part of the Barton family. Always. Always." Adeline clung to his neck, the checked tears now falling in torrents. William tenderly released the young girl's hold and slowly walked back to the wagon, leaving her forlorn and alone on the stoop.

She watched as Joseph guided the departing wagon and its inhabitants on to Stewart's Flat one-and-only boarding house. As the schooner meandered around the bend, the canopy slowly dipped below the hill's crest, disappearing from her sight. She remained still, envisioning where the wagon had been, wishing that she could be back on the

Strangers and Sojourners in a Town Called Penryn:

ADELINE

plains, traveling with her family—contented, accepted, needed, loved. She made no movement towards the back door. Instead, she gazed past the line of trees and brushes and stared at the full moon that seemed to sit on the horizon like a lone bird perched on a sprawling tree branch. Spotting the silhouette of a large granite mound, she moved towards it, resting there for a moment to think on the last ten months of her life. She looked up through the tree branches, gazed at the full moon and began to sing the only song that spoke her heart.

When I be far from home,
When I be far from home,
When I be far from home,
Gib me Jesus.

Her former servant family was far away, a lingering memory. But this forced and undesired exodus had given her a glimpse and a hope of a different life. Before entering her new place of servitude, she offered a simple praise to the heavens. "Thank you, Jesus, that my new fam'ly be so close."

Strangers and Sojourners in a Town Called Penryn:

ADELINE

Chapter 7

*In peace I will lie down and sleep;
for you alone, O Lord, make me to dwell in safety.
Psalm 4:8*

**Stewart's Flat, California
October 1853**

Adeline, accustomed to rising before dawn, awoke to unfamiliar accommodations. The morning light entering through the window gave a clearer picture of the bedroom's contents. Last night, the full moon had cast its silver beams on her sleeping quarters, but Adeline could only see the outline of the bed. Now she saw the beauty of the multi-colored crazy quilt that kept her warm through the night. A small, black, barrel-top trunk sat at the foot of the bed. Opposite the bed stood a plain chest of drawers, its top adorned with an ordinary off-white wash basin, pitcher, linen towel, and a bar of all-purpose lye soap. An unadorned, six-paned window shared the wall with the dresser along with the door that opened to the back porch stoop.

Strangers and Sojourners in a Town Called Penryn:

ADELINE

Lastly, opposite the door and at the foot of the trunk, rose the steep stairs to the attic loft. Adeline calculated the size of the room by using her small feet as a measuring tool. As she walked the length, she counted, "One, two, three, four. . . .25." Then the width. "One, two, three, four. . .20." She stopped and looked the room over again, pleased with her surroundings. *My! It be bigger than my room back in Mississip'. But no need for me to get attached to this room since I 'prob'ly be living up in the loft 'ventually."* Outloud, she reminded herself, "Know where your place be, Adeline." Glancing up to the attic space, she repeated, "Know where your place be."

She unpacked her bag, placing her much too few belongings in the dresser. After making up the bed, she washed and dried her face and hands. She then turned towards the second door in the room—the one that led to the main living area. Quietly opening it an inch at a time, she cautiously peeked into the outer living room. A brown and blue woven rug covered nearly the entire floor. At the corners of the rug, in front of the fireplace, sat two upholstered

Strangers and Sojourners in a Town Called Penryn:

ADELINE

and embroidered rocking chairs. They faced the fireplace ready to receive the owners of the house.

The fireplace still held last night's now dormant embers. Adeline found the fireplace poker and stirred up the dwindling coals, encouraging them to flare up. She added several logs from the indoor woodpile stack. They smoldered a bit, then caught fire.

Satisfied with her efforts, she turned her attention to the rest of the room. A large dark blue settee graced the middle of the room and also faced the fireplace. Though not as pretty as the rocking chairs, its luxurious fabric and gold fringe spoke of money and privilege.

Behind the couch, at the back of the room, loomed an over-sized dining table. Four straight-backed chairs graced the side of the table that was closest to Adeline. On the other side was a settle which matched the length of the table. Adeline ran her hand over the smooth, polished tabletop then across the tops of the chairs. *Such simple things, but they is so pretty.*

To her wonder, what appeared to be a large landscape painting on the wall behind the dining table was actually

Strangers and Sojourners in a Town Called Penryn:

ADELINE

two massive windows whose trim showcased the outdoor scenery much like a gilded frame enhanced the beauty of a Rembrandt masterpiece.

She moved quietly towards the stove—an immense, five burner, coal black fixture that swallowed up the back of the room. Its most noticeable features were decorative silver embellishments; the handles, grates, legs, and edges were a lustrous, gleaming silver. A mahogany hoosier set next to the the stove, its silver knobs and pulls matched the brilliance the stove's. The morning sunlight rays, reflected by the shininess of the metal pieces, bounced onto the opposite wall, creating an indoor rainbow.

Bewitched by the sight, Adeline took no notice of Mary entering the room. A forced cough broke the spell.

Adeline turned towards the sound. Mary stood at her bedroom door. Adeline remained silent, waiting for her mistress to address her.

"I see that you survived your journey, Adeline. Your arrival is timely as I am becoming a bit cumbersome in doing the chores."

Strangers and Sojourners in a Town Called Penryn:

ADELINE

"Oh, I, I, I, . . " Adeline could not stop gawking at her mistress.

"Quit stammering, Adeline. I am sure that you have seen many women in my condition. Don't be so surprised."

"Yes'm. It be, jes', well, it jes' be so soon!"

Mary harrumphed. "Not soon enough. December is still two months away."

"Yes'm. I guess we still gots time to get things ready for the baby."

"Yes, Adeline, we will be busy. Come. Let me show you what needs to be done."

Strangers and Sojourners in a Town Called Penryn:

ADELINE

Chapter 8

I will never leave you nor forsake you.
Hebrews 13:5

Quite quickly, Adeline's weekday routines became a sort of physical sing-song to her. *Rise up with chick'ns. Collect eggs. Milk cow. Stoke fire. Boil wadder. Make brekfist. Clean dishes. Clean house. Clean clothes. Sew baby clothes. Make dinner. Make supper. Feed an'mals.'Adeline, do this. Adeline do that. Adeline, speak up! Adeline, shush up!'* But Sunday. Oh, blessed Sunday!

Early every sabbath morning, Adeline positioned herself on the large granite boulder behind the house and waited patiently for Mr. William. Sometimes she would rise up two hours before the scheduled time just to enjoy this quiet day. No hammering miners, no clanging blacksmith, no resounding school bells; all workday noises replaced by the birds' chirping, the rivulet's tumbling, and the cows' lowing. The peacefulness of the morning signaled a day of rest for Adeline--a day to spend with her adopted family.

Strangers and Sojourners in a Town Called Penryn:

ADELINE

This time of interlude also had its routines. Wake up early. Wait for Mr. William. Watch the road for the wagon. Wend the way back to the boarding house. Wave at impatient 'Lia, looking out from the window, waiting for her "Addy." Wander through the town with Miz Catheraine and 'Lia. Adeline wide-eyed at the new buildings and businesses that seemed to spring up in just a week's time. Their walks, at first, garnered questioning looks from other passersby. But gradually, the town folks grew accustomed to seeing the two disparate Sunday walkers with the lovely 'Lia waddling between them.

"Miz Cathy, when you and Mr. William be building a place of your own?"

"Well, probably in the next year or two. I am still a bit weary from our journey and William thought it best to wait until I am a bit stronger. The boarding house suits us fine for now. Living here saves me from doing the cleaning and cooking that a regular home requires, allowing me to spend my time and energy on my little Annelia."

They both looked down at the energetic child toddling between them. Adeline reached for her hand to steady

Strangers and Sojourners in a Town Called Penryn:

ADELINE

the child. 'Lia would have none of it. She batted at Adeline's hand. "M'sef. Do m'sef.!"

Catheraine tried to catch her daughter from falling, causing 'Lia to cry out even louder, **"No! Do m'sef!"**

"Gracious. I declares little Missy. You be one right stubborn chile'."

"You are so right, Addie. She is barely 19 months old but has the determination of an adult. I fear we might have a bit of trouble with her in a few years."

"Don't be aworrying, Miz Cathy. We both be there to gib her direction. She cain't fight

both of us!"

Laughing, they each clasped one of 'Lia's hands and firmly directed the young girl,

together reciting their own version of Proverbs 22:6. "Train up *Annelia* in the way she

should go: and when Annelia is old, she will not depart from it."

Sundays always ended with a sit-down meal at the boarding house. Once a week, Adeline would be the served, instead of the server. At the end of the meal, the Barton

Strangers and Sojourners in a Town Called Penryn:

ADELINE

family would then gave thanks aloud; firstly, William; secondly, Catheraine; and lastly, Adeline. This Sunday night continued the pattern.

"Father in heaven, thank You for the love bestowed to us. Thank You for the ones given
to us. Thank you for the time provided to us. Amen."

"Heavenly Father, all good things come from You. In your time, all things are made beautiful. May my time on earth be spent honoring You. Amen."

"Lord Jesus, I be blest by this fam'ly. I be blest by all d' love giv'n to dis servant girl. Help me be a blessin' to others. Amen."

"Do m'sef! Do m'sef!" 'Lia brought the palms of her tiny hands together, raised them to her face, bowed her head upon them, and boldly bellowed her prayer. "Mmm-mmm, Mama; Mmmmm Papa; Mmmm Ad'line. Ah-h-h-h--men."

The other diners in the boarding house turned and smiled at the endearing little girl. Catheraine covered her cheeks with her hands, hiding the pink blushing that had suddenly appeared. Unembarrassed, William swooped up

Strangers and Sojourners in a Town Called Penryn:

ADELINE

the child, chuckling at his daughter's boldness. Bowing to the captive audience, he declared, "Amen" and left the dining hall with Catheraine and Adeline following closely behind.

William fetched the horse and wagon. Adeline gathered her things, gave good-bye kisses and hugs to Catheraine and 'Lia, then waited on the front porch of the boarding house for her transportation back to the Goldstan household. Her most favorite day's routines joyfully completed.

Strangers and Sojourners in a Town Called Penryn:

ADELINE

Chapter 9

*When the cares of my heart are many,
your consolations cheer my soul.
Psalm 94:19*

As the weeks of fall passed, Adeline's work hours expanded in direct correlation to Miss Mary's ever-expanding midsection. The more Mary filled out, the more assistance she required from Adeline; from getting out of bed, putting on her stockings, buttoning her shoes, to helping her walk the uneven pathway to the privy. Adeline endured it all. What else could she do? This was why she had been brought to California. Soon, she would be taking care of an infant as well.

Winter arrived early but not like the roaring rainfall so common to Lafayette Springs, Mississippi. Instead, gentle showers and soft breezes graced the inhabitants of Stewart's Flat. Mary grew restless, restricted by the intermittent drops and by her motherly condition, demanding more assistance from her young domestic.

Strangers and Sojourners
in a Town Called Penryn:

ADELINE

During her last week of her confinement, Mary had insisted Joseph hire a midwife to stay at the house. She midwife arrived on Sunday, December 11, while Adeline was away at her weekly visit with the Bartons.

As with every Sunday night after the family dinner, Mr. William delivered Adeline to her backdoor stoop. This Sunday night was no different. Adeline waved good-bye, turned and opened the door to "her" room, and entered as quietly as possible so as not to disturb Mary and Joseph in the other room. But her intentions of being silent vanished as she gasped, "OH, OH, MY GRACIOUS!! Who you be. . .?", while at the same time the room's newly acquired inhabitant uttered the almost exact same words.

"'Scuse me, ma'am. Sorry to of scared you. I knowed you be acomin' 'cept I forgit you be acomin' dis evenin'. You done took me by 'sprize. I be Adeline, Miz Mary's servant."

The startled woman bristled at Adeline. "Well, I must say that you gave me a fright."

Adeline lowered her eyes. "Yes'm. I'll just git my things and sleep in the loft."

Strangers and Sojourners in a Town Called Penryn:

ADELINE

"No need to rummage through the dresser. Mary has already put your things in your carpetbag. She placed it at the foot of the ladder."

"Yes'm. Thank you, um, um. . ."

"You may address me as Miss Lydia."

"Yes'm. Thank you, Miz Lydia. Goodnight then."

Adeline picked up her well-used traveling bag, took up one of the two lighted pewter candlesticks perched on the dresser, and slowly made her way up the ladder. Her dress hindered forward progress so much that in exasperation, she hurled the bag carrying all of her meager worldly possessions through the opening in the loft at the top of the ladder. With her now-free hand, she hiked up the dress, finished climbing the steps, and crossed the threshold into the upstairs living quarters. Last week, upon Mary's instructions, Adeline had cleaned the dusty catch-all attic space. Standing at the top of the ladder, she scrutinized her handiwork.

The loft size adequately met Adeline's needs, although the head space along the side walls was a bit low. The entire floor area measured the same space as the two

**Strangers and Sojourners
in a Town Called Penryn:**

ADELINE

bedrooms situated directly below the loft. A few trunks and miscellaneous household items neatly occupied a corner of the room. Adeline stepped up into the room and placed the flickering candle on a gray flattop trunk. Next to the trunk lay a thick straw-stuffed burlap pallet covered with a flannel sheet and patchwork quilt. A small down pillow graced the head of the pad. The bed's placement under the end apex of the ceiling and the ventilation window allowed a small amount of light to shine on the sleeping area and allowed fresh air to circulate in the attic space. The chimney wall radiated heat throughout the sparsely appointed room. A dainty sewing rocker completed Adeline's furnishings. Pegs for clothing lined a wall plank. Adeline unpacked her few things, hanging them on the dowels. Resting in the compact rocking chair, Adeline bowed her head. "Thank you, Jesus, for my very own place. I be blest onced agin. My new prayer be that one day, my Barton family and my place be together under the same roof. Amen."

On Friday, December 16, 1853, Adeline gained another task to add to her daily routines; Thomas Sierra

Strangers and Sojourners in a Town Called Penryn:

ADELINE

Nevada Goldstan began his life at Stewart's Flat—the first baby born into the growing township.

The midwife vacated the Goldstan household a week after the birthing. Before departing, she gave Adeline strict instructions on how to care for the new mother and baby Thomas, stressing the necessity of rest for the two patients.

Adeline chose to remain in the loft, knowing that the bedroom would eventually belong to baby Thomas.

***

"Such a long-handled name. *Thomas Sierra Nevada Goldstan.* I declare! Why you 'spose they named him that? Miz Cathy." Adeline held 'Lia firmly on her lap, brushing the restless girl's hair.

Catheraine chuckled a bit to herself. Putting her fingers to her lips, she gazed upward, as if the answer would appear on the ceiling of her boarding house room. After a bit of contemplation, she turned her face back to Adeline.

"Adeline, do you know about babies. . .I mean. . .do you know how. . .know how babies come to be?"

Strangers and Sojourners in a Town Called Penryn:

ADELINE

"Oh, Miz Cathy, you cain't be a slave 'n not know! Quarters be so close 'n all. It be a part of life, babies 'n such."

"Well, since you are aware of this fact of life, then let me see if you can figure out why Joseph and Mary named their baby the way they did. I'll give you some clues and you try and guess."

"First of all, the first name, Thomas."

"Oh, that be the easy part. That baby be named after Miz Mary's favorite brother, Thomas."

"Correct, Addie. Now, let's get to his middle names. While you traveled in a wagon to come to California, Mary and Joseph traveled to California *by* ? ? ?"

Adeline's faced beamed. She knew the story by heart. She had eavesdropped on Mary's conversations with the local womenfolk who had come avisiting.

"First, after the weddin' they goes to New York City for a time; then, they goes by a steamer ship to Panama; 'n then they traipse across that whole God-forsaken country, (Miz Mary's 'xact words), clean to the other side of it and wind up at 'nother ocean; they git on 'nother steamer ship

Strangers and Sojourners in a Town Called Penryn:

ADELINE

and fine'ly ends up in San Fran Cis co! 'n then they travel by wagon to Stewart's Flat."

"Well, Adeline, suppose I tell you that the last steamship that Joseph and Mary traveled on was called the *Sierra Nevada*. Would that give you a clue as to why they named their baby Sierra Nevada?"

Adeline thought a bit, then a bit more. She rolled her eyes, giggled a little, and looked conspiratorially at Catheraine. Her giggling turned into full-fledged laughter. "Why, Miz Cathy, that baby come about while they be on that ship!"

Laughing just as loudly as Adeline, Catheraine confirmed the obvious. "You are right, Addie. You are so right!"

'Lia, seeing tears roll down both of their faces, began to whimper.

Both Catheraine and Adeline tried to comfort the worried child but still could not contain their own tears of laughter, causing 'Lia to cry along with them.

Strangers and Sojourners in a Town Called Penryn:

ADELINE

Chapter 10

*Six days you shall do your work,
but on the seventh day you shall rest;
. . .that the son of your servant woman,
and the alien, may be refreshed.
Exodus 23:12*

Sundays were not only a time of refreshing for Adeline, they were also a time of refining. Besides learning about the bible and memorizing bible verses, Miss Cathy also gently schooled Adeline in the way that she should talk. "Be" was especially troublesome for Adeline. As she would start to relate her week's happenings to Catheraine with "I be so busy", a "hmmmm?" would be voiced by her teacher. Adeline would stop, pause, think about all the ways that "be" should be used, choose the one that should go with "I', and started again.

"I *am* so busy, I hardly be able,". . . "Hmmmmmm?" interrupted Catheraine, again. Another pause from Adeline.

"I *am* so busy, I hardly *am* able to get time enough for the privy! There, I done it right!!"

Strangers and Sojourners in a Town Called Penryn:

ADELINE

"Yes, you **are** doing much better, Addie. I know you think that this **is** a waste of time, but I only want what **is** best for you."

"Yes, ma'am. I surely **am** pleased that you **are** learning me to speak proper."

"Well, Addie, it is a joy to watch you blossom in all your ways. You are growing up right before my eyes, just like 'Lia. Can you believe that she will soon be two years old in March? And that you will be nine in April?" Catheraine paused. She gazed at 'Lia then at Adeline. Taking Adeline's hand, she continued on. "There is still so much for you to learn. I only wish that I had permission to teach you how to read and write. Perhaps one day."

"Yes'm. I be here for you to teach me when the time be right."

"Again, Adeline."

"Mmmm. . .I **am** here for you to teach me when the time **is** right."

"Much better. No more lessons today. Let's go down to the parlor. Dinner should be ready soon."

Strangers and Sojourners in a Town Called Penryn:

ADELINE

As Adeline carried 'Lia down the stairs, Catheraine and William followed a ways behind. Still, she was able to hear bits and pieces of their conversation.

"William, you have to tell her. She needs to know."

"I know Cathy. I'll tell her soon—when the time is right."

"There will never be a right time, William. The longer you wait, the more difficult it will become."

"Yes, dear."

After dinner, Adeline and William settled into the wagon seat and headed back to the Goldstan house. This return journey always seemed to come too soon for Adeline. But each Sunday spent with laughter and love soothed her weariness and rejuvenated her for the upcoming week ahead. Her soul was satisfied, for at least another week.

William halted the wagon at the back of the house. He helped Adeline down from the bench, giving her a hug as he placed her securely on the ground.

"Addie, do you know what is happening next Sunday?"

Strangers and Sojourners in a Town Called Penryn:

ADELINE

"Um, the same as this Sunday?"

"Yes, it will be a visiting day for you. But, next Sunday is also Christmas Day."

Adeline's eyes grew large with excitement. "Truly, Mr. William? It be Christmas? I mean, it is Christmas Day? I ain't never had a real Christmas! Truly?"

"Truly. Maybe this week will not seem so tedious. You have something extra special to think about to help you through all your chores. Now, go inside before you catch cold."

"Yes, Mr. William. I be. . .I **am** so excited for next Sunday."

As William drove away, Adeline looked up in wonderment to the stars, just as the Magi must have done so many years before. She whispered into the still, starry, December night. "I be having me a real Christmas."

Throughout that week, Adeline rushed through her chores. While baby Thomas (and Miss Mary) napped, Adeline used the time to make presents for her Sunday family. With her mistress's permission, she assembled scraps of

Strangers and Sojourners in a Town Called Penryn:

ADELINE

material leftover from Thomas's layette to construct a rag doll for 'Lia. Once the body of the doll was completed, Adeline concentrated on the clothing.

Using a piece of blue cotton chambray, she fashioned a dainty apron for the doll to go over its white muslin dress. Next, a bit of black twilled cotton served as the material for the hi-top shoes. Adeline sewed the booties onto the doll's feet. For the dolly's hair, Adeline gathered a piece of sheep's wool that she had found caught on a neighbor's fencing. She scrubbed the wool with lye soap, making sure that it was as clean as possible then placed the fluff of wool in a cast iron pot of boiling setting solution--water and vinegar. After an hour, she removed the pot from the stove, allowed the water to cool, took out the wool, and squeezed out all the excess moisture. While the wool dried, Adeline prepared the dye, using the Goldstan's kitchen supply of dried dandelion flower heads--again with Miss Mary's permission.

Adeline filled the same small pot with the dandelion heads, covered the flowers with water, then set the pot back on the stove to bring this mixture to a boil. Once it began to

Strangers and Sojourners in a Town Called Penryn:

ADELINE

boil, she lowered the heat, lidded the pot, and let the dye simmer for two hours. Checking that the color was just right, she strained the mixture into a bowl, added the dried piece of wool to the golden liquid, covered the bowl with a dinner plate, and placed it on a shelf in the pie safe to let the woolen "hair" steep overnight. The next day, Adeline sewed the golden blonde hair onto the doll, parted the wool down the middle of the head, plaited two braids, then secured their ends with strips of blue gingham material. Rehydrated blackberry juice supplied the eye's coloring, lovingly smudged by Adeline's pointer finger. She rubbed fleshy pomegranate seeds on the muslin to create lips. Lastly, she carefully embroidered around the eyes and lips, added eye brows and two dimples, completing the doll's facial features.

Once the doll was finished, Adeline turned her attention to making William's gift, again using Miss Mary's cast-off scraps of material. Taking all the skinny leftover cut strips of woolen cloth, she patch-worked them together, creating a multi-colored piece of material approximately four feet long and six inches wide. Threading an embroi-

Strangers and Sojourners in a Town Called Penryn:

ADELINE

dery needle with a heavy yellow strand of cotton yarn, she blanket stitched a border around all the edges. Next, she cross-stitched around all the patch-work pieces, using different colored yarns for each patch. When all the sewing was completed, Adeline laid her handiwork on her bed. "Yep, that be a fine scarf. Jus' right for Mr. William. Now, I jus' gots Miss Cathy left to do."

Adeline lay awake the whole night. *Only two more days 'til Sunday. What can I give Miss Cathy? The tiny bird's nest I found is nice but is it special enough? It gots to be sump'in extry special, sump'in to show just how much I love her. Some part of me that she can always have with her, no matters what be. Dear Jesus, please show me.*

That evening, as Adeline lay wide awake in the loft, she overheard Mary and Joseph talking about their plans for Christmas.

"How I wish Mother and Father could be with us. Little Thomas's first Christmas and no one here to celebrate. I so want my family to see our baby."

Strangers and Sojourners in a Town Called Penryn:

ADELINE

"Mary, we can celebrate together, just our little family. Then maybe this summer, after your strength returns and Thomas is a little older, you can travel back to Mississippi for a visit. How would you like that? The trip will be my Christmas present to you."

"Oh, Joseph. Thank you for your thoughtfulness, but I will not go unless you go with me. Those three years you spent out here without me were the loneliest years of my life and I never want to be apart from you again." I will travel back to Mississippi for a visit only if you are with me.

The continuing conversation turned into soft murmurs, indistinguishable to Adeline.

***

After a fitful night's sleep, Adeline arose earlier than usual. She went quietly about her chores so as not to disturb the still sleeping baby and his birth-weary nursing mother.

Joseph had already left the house to attend to his daily job overseeing the duties at the mine. Adeline knew his morning routine would take about two hours to complete. This gave her time to prepare the morning meal before he

Strangers and Sojourners
in a Town Called Penryn:

ADELINE

came back. By the time she gathered the eggs, milked the cow, and started the coffee, Joseph would be done with his rounds and be back home to breakfast with Mary. If 'lil Thomas was awake, Joseph would gently rock him until the infant fell asleep for his morning nap.

Afterwards, while Adeline kept busy caring for Mary and baby Thomas, Joseph would stay nearby, working the rest of the day on the farm—feeding the livestock, mending the fences, plotting the layout of the upcoming spring garden.

This particular morning Joseph brought a surprise back to the house—a letter from Mary's mother. Adeline dragged her feet in cleaning the breakfast dishes, pots, and pans. She wanted to hear about her old home.

"Oh, Joseph! God must have known how homesick I was!" Mary hugged her husband, then sat in the rocker by the fireplace. She hurriedly opened the envelope, reading the contents of the letter to herself. Every now and then she read aloud to Joseph the parts that he might be interested in. "Mmmm. . .everyone is doing well. . .mama says that our departure was providential as yellow fever was especially

**Strangers and Sojourners
in a Town Called Penryn:**

ADELINE

fierce this last summer, especially in New Orleans. . .cotton prices were at their highest. . .good crop harvested. . .Wait. What's this?"

Tucked inside the envelope was a lock of hair, tied together with a pink ribbon. "Oh, Joseph, look!" Mary held up the wispy symbol of unending love and devotion. "A lock of mother's hair! She must have sensed my longing for her. Just touching its softness brings her closer to me."

Mary lowered her head, her tears falling on the letter. As Joseph comforted Mary, Adeline raised her eyes to the ceiling. *Thank you, Jesus. I knows what to give to Miss Cathy.*

Strangers and Sojourners in a Town Called Penryn:

ADELINE

Chapter 11

*A gift opens the way for the giver
and ushers him into the presence of the great.
Proverbs 18:16*

Yuletide 1853

*Christmas day! I, hmm, **am** so, so, so happy!* Adeline's cheerfulness could not be contained. She sat beside William and tried to contain her excitement. The crisp, clear, cold December morning's glimmering sunlight mirrored Addie's radiant smile. On her lap perched a medium-sized straw basket, the contents concealed with a lace-edged hand towel. She slapped William's hand away as he tried to catch of peek of the contents.

"So tell me, Addie, what is in your basket?"

"Oh, Mr. William, it be, I means, it **is** a s'prize!" Adeline hugged the basket close to her. "After all, it **is** Christmas!"

Strangers and Sojourners in a Town Called Penryn:

ADELINE

The usual order of the Sunday activities were reversed for Christmas. First, everyone in the boarding house gathered for a grand noontime holiday feast. And what a feast! The side-boards groaned under the weight of the food. Roasted beef, wild turkey, and goose; mince pies, with their combination of savory meet and sweet apples; star-gazy pies, where the whole baked fish stared upwards to the heavens from its casserole tin; potatoes, whipped and piled high as a mountain with fresh churned butter streaming down the sides like the snowmelt in springtime; fresh dandelion greens, skillet cooked with bacon and onions; turnips; parsnips; pickled beets; pickled pigs' feet. And fresh baked rolls! The aromas of each dish wafted to the sky, offering up themselves as a sacrifice to this special day.

Adeline stood in wonderment at the sight. She then spotted the sideboard full of desserts; Christmas cookies and pudding, apple brown betty, peach cobbler, blackberry pie, and candy canes. And at the end of the sweets, an immense glass punch bowl, filled to the brim with frothy eggnog.

Strangers and Sojourners in a Town Called Penryn:

ADELINE

"My, oh my, oh my."

Catheraine smiled at Adeline and placed her arm around the open-mouthed girl.

"Merry first *real* Christmas with our family, my sweet Adeline."

After the noonday repast, the Barton family returned to their upstairs living quarters. 'Lia rested in Adeline's arms as Addie gently rocked her, the crackling fireplace lulling the child and nanny into a late afternoon, after-meal nap. Catheraine laid 'Lia in the child's bed, covering her with a woolen blanket. She then placed a coverlet over Adeline, causing the happily exhausted eight-year-old to stir slightly. To William and Catheraine, she appeared to be asleep. In fact, she had awakened when Catheraine covered her but was so warm and comfortable that she remained in a dream-like state. As she drowsed, the whispered conversation between the married couple sounded muffled and far away.

"William, you must promise me that you will watch after her when I am gone."

Strangers and Sojourners in a Town Called Penryn:

ADELINE

"Cathy, there is no reason to talk of this. The doctor said that you were doing better. You are feeling better, aren't you?"

"Some days, yes. Others, well, on the others it takes all my strength just to get out of bed.
It is no different than when we lived back home. Good days. Bad days. I always felt that 'Lia and I should have stayed behind. At least my parents would have been able to care for Annelia after I am gone. Perhaps we... *I* should go back."

William's back stiffened. His next words, harshly and angrily whispered. "You are not going back. I will not be kept apart from you, no matter how ill you may become. You know I only elected to this move for your well-being since California's weather is more conducive to your condition. You must hold on to life. You must try." These last words were barely discernible, spoken through William's raspy sobs.

Catherine's touch soothed his crying. "Promise me to watch over her." Promise me you will do everything in your

Strangers and Sojourners
in a Town Called Penryn:

ADELINE

power to protect Adeline. She will need you as much as Annelia will need you."

Upon hearing her name, Adeline wakened, yawned, and stretched her arms. She was not quite sure if the dream had called her name or if it had truly been spoken aloud by either Catheraine or William. The couple glanced at Adeline—their private discussion silenced by Adeline's awakening. Addie looked from one staring adult to the other, not sure of what was happening.

"Everything be. . .I mean, Everything *is* fine?"

"**Is** everything fine?" modeled Catheraine. "Yes, Addie, everything is quite fine. Let's awaken 'Lia. It is time for presents."

Adeline's brown leather lacing boots fit perfectly. She proudly displayed her gift, walking back and forth across the living area. While walking, she held both hands out, as if waving to passersby, with her fawn colored lamb skin gloves. Such luxuries!

"Oh, Miz Cathy, Mr. William. They be beautiful!"

"Yes, Adeline, they *be* beautiful."

Hugs and kisses. Kisses and hugs.

Strangers and Sojourners in a Town Called Penryn:

ADELINE

"Now, Miz Cathy, Mr. William, 'Lia. My turn to give the presents. First, Mr. William."

Adeline handed the wrapped gift to a surprised William.

"Why, Addie, you didn't have to give me anything."

"I knows it, Mr. William. But I wanted to. You and Miz Cathy, you be my fam'ly."

"Thank you, Adeline." William slowly unwrapped the package. He held up the scarf of many colors for all to see then wrapped it around his neck.

"Such a work of art! And so warm. This will surely keep out the cold. Thank you, Addie."

Adeline beamed. How words of praise make glad the heart.

"Next, Missy 'Lia."

'Lia's not-quite-two-year-old fingers fumbled with the wrapping strings. Finally, with a little help from her mother, she uncovered her doll.

"Baby! Mama. . ." she tugged on Catheraine's dress, holding up the dolly, "Baby! Baby 'Lia!"

Strangers and Sojourners in a Town Called Penryn:

ADELINE

"Yes, 'Lia, it does look like you. Thank you Addie. It is the perfect gift for her."

Adeline shyly handed the last remaining gift to Catheraine.

As Catheraine removed the last of the wrapping, she brought her hand up to her mouth. Tears began to fall. She cradled a small bird's nest in her other hand. Inside were three round, smooth, white stones and one jagged black stone. Nestled under the rough black stone was a tendril of Adeline's molasses colored hair, the strands held together with a burlap string. Catheraine gathered Adeline in her arms. "Yes, my rough-edged little black angel, you are a part of our nest, our family, forever and ever, no matter what may come to pass."

'Lia sat wedged between Addie and her papa. Normally, riding in the wagon so late in the evening would have been out of the question for the youngster. However, because of her heartfelt supplication, "Wanna go too, Papa, wanna go toooooo!" no one could say 'no' to her. So, Catheraine and Adeline bundled her up with two sweaters

Strangers and Sojourners in a Town Called Penryn:

ADELINE

and an overcoat; pulled woolen mittens over her hands, guiding the tiny thumbs into their correct spot; laced up her high-top boots; covered her head and ears with a knitted stocking cap then sent her merrily out the door, hand-in-hand with Adeline and Papa.

The clear night sky, a dark purple-blue in appearance, served as a back-drop to the silver winter stars. 'Lia began counting them. "One, two, free, four, five, six, seben, ten, 'leven, fifteen, nineteen, hunred! A hunred stars!"

"Twinkle, twinkle, little star," William and Adeline sang with gusto. "How I wonder what you are. Up above the world so high, like a diamond in the sky,'" Lia joined in on the chorus. *"Twinkle, twinkle little star, how I wonder what you are."*

'Lia did not know the remaining verses, but would join in on the refrain after each verse had been sung.

"When the blazing sun is gone, when he nothing shines upon, then you show your little light, twinkle, twinkle, all the night. . ."

"Twinkle, twinkle little star, how I wonder what you are."

Strangers and Sojourners in a Town Called Penryn:

ADELINE

"Then the traveller in the dark, thanks you for your tiny spark, he could not see which way to go, if you did not twinkle so. . ."

"Twinkle, twinkle little star, how I wonder what you are."

"In the dark blue sky you keep, and often through my curtains peep, for you never shut your eye, 'till the sun is in the sky. . ."

"Twinkle, twinkle little star, how I wonder what you are."

"As your bright and tiny spark, lights the traveller in the dark, though I know not what you are, twinkle, twinkle, little star. . ."

"Twinkle, twinkle little star, how I wonder what you are."

The trio arrived at the Goldstan house just as the they sang the last 'are', holding out this final word as long as their lungs would allow. After all breath was exhausted, they concluded their performance with a spirited round of clapping and whistling. Joseph and Mary, hearing the ruckus, opened their front door to welcome in the im-

Strangers and Sojourners in a Town Called Penryn:

ADELINE

promptu carolers. Adeline started to go around to the back, to her doorway, but William caught her hand, brought her alongside 'Lia and ushered her into the front parlor.

"Merry Christmas, Joe and Mary, oh, and little Thomas." William stooped down and gently touched the barely-week-old baby boy, lying in his cradle. 'Lia came near her Papa, wanting to see the baby. She, too, tenderly caressed his cheek, mimicking her Papa's action. William gathered 'Lia closer, hugging her with a fierceness that she didn't understand. She squirmed out of his embrace but stayed by his side. William turned and chuckled at Joseph.

"He is a beautiful baby, Joseph. Takes after Mary's side of the family!"

After a few more minutes of visiting, William and 'Lia said their good-byes and headed back to the boarding house. Joseph, Mary, and Thomas settled into their bedroom. Adeline ascended to her loft. And Christmas departed until the next year.

Strangers and Sojourners in a Town Called Penryn:

ADELINE

Chapter 12

*When the cares of my heart are many,
your consolations cheer my soul.
Psalm 94:19*

Adeline's daily and weekly routines carried on. Two full years of the four seasons came and went. She lovingly watched as 'Lia grew and flourished, the child's progress contrasting sharply with Catheraine's health that seemed to dwindle and weaken with each passing day--despite the good weather of California, despite the Doctor's assurances that she was on the mend.

William had never told Adeline about Catheraine's lingering illness--consumption, but Adeline had guessed it some time ago. Her Sunday visits now became more focused on caring for Miss Cathy while William would entertain 'Lia. Finally, on a Sunday visit in November of 1855, while William and 'Lia were downstairs in the boardinghouse parlor, Adeline could not help but confess to Catheraine.

Strangers and Sojourners in a Town Called Penryn:

ADELINE

"I know you are sick, Miss Cathy. I know that you and Mr. William tried to tell me a long time ago. . .but just wernt able. But I done known for quite some time. I be here for you whenever you need me. I be here until. . .until. . .you no longer be with me." Her voice trailed off.

Catheraine, appearing asleep, heard every word. She gently placed her pale, white, trembling hand on Adeline's steady strong hand. She did not open her eyes but spoke softly—a mere whisper. "I love you, my brown-skinned daughter Adeline. Adeline Barton." She then slept, her hand still resting on Adeline's.

***

January 6, 1856 fell on a Sunday. Normally, Sundays found Adeline up and ready before dawn's first light with an eagerness to join her family. But not this Sunday.

Miss Mary's second pregnancy was not going as easy as her first, requiring her to depend on Adeline even more. The previous day had been so tiresome for Adeline that the

Strangers and Sojourners in a Town Called Penryn:

ADELINE

remaining strength she did have was expended on just crawling up the loft and into bed, fully clothed.

Now, someone had disturbed her much needed slumber. She looked out the dormer window. *The moon be high. Not even near mornin' time. What is so dang impor'ent that it cain't wait a few more hours? And why the infernal tappin', tappin, tappin' on my back door, 'stead of the front? Well, at least I don't have t' get dressed.* She clambered down the ladder, careful to not miss a step.

Opening the back door, she welcomed the intruder with a quiet but forceful "Shu-u-u-sh. There be a baby sleepin' here!"

The moonlight at the back of the night guest cast his face in darkness. But Adeline knew who it belonged to by the outline framed by the moon's glow. She quietly affirmed the visitor with a solemn, "Mr. William."

"It's time, Adeline. She wants to see you before. . .before. . ."

Adeline slipped on her walking shoes and gently grasped William's large calloused right hand with her small,

Strangers and Sojourners in a Town Called Penryn:

ADELINE

equally calloused, left hand. "It be all right, Mr. William. It be all right."

She left him to inform Mary of the situation. Minutes later she carefully and quietly closed the door and joined William on the back door stoop. They started toward the still slumbering town. Together, they began a journey that neither one wanted to travel.

***

Adeline tried to straighten up the room quietly but the least little noise seemed to cause Miss Catheraine to stir in her bed, so she decided just to sit still and concentrate on darning 'Lia's socks. As her hands worked methodically at the sewing, her thoughts drifted back to her first night in Stewart's Flat.

It be almost three years ago, I sat on a granite boulder, staring up at a starry sky, a skinny little eight-year-old slave pickaninny afraid of this new life chosen for me. Baby Thomas was born during my first year here. Now, right shortly, a second Goldstan baby be coming. I may be only nearly eleven-years-old, but I can take care of babies just as good as grown-ups can. Bless the good Lord, if it twern't

Strangers and Sojourners in a Town Called Penryn:

ADELINE

for my learning from Miss Catheraine and practicing on Missy 'Lia, I wouldn't have known nothing 'bout takin' care of babies.

She picked another sock out of the darning basket and selected a coordinating thread. *'Lia, such a big girl, almost-four years-old! I never seen such a strong-headed little gal. When she wants sumptin' she sure makes it known to anyone within hollerin' distance.*

A faint moan interrupted Adeline's thoughts. She put down her mending and moved to the bed, recovering Catheraine with a heavy quilt. Taking a washcloth from the bedside table, Adeline dipped it in the water bowl, squeezed out the excess, then placed it on her adopted mother's forehead. With what little strength she had, Catheraine lifted her arm and placed her hand over Adeline's hand. "Thank you, my angel sent from above."

Adeline encompassed Catheraine's hand with her own. She bent down, gently kissed the dying woman's cheek and whispered, "Good-bye my mama, my friend. I will always 'member you."

Strangers and Sojourners in a Town Called Penryn:

ADELINE

Catheraine nodded, closed her eyes for the last time, and entered into her eternal sleep.

Adeline dropped her head in prayer and grief. . .William's long ago sermon recalled to her mind. "*A time to be born, and a time to die."*

She walked slowly out onto the hallway landing just as William and 'Lia were coming up the stairwell. The eleven-year-old raised her tear-stained face up to William. Not a word passed between them—the unspoken news evident in the salty stream rolling down Adeline's cheeks. William drew her to him, consoling her as best as he could while he took slow, deep breaths in an effort to keep himself from weeping. 'Lia, too young to understand, looked to Adeline. "Is Mama more sick?"

"No, chile', your mama not be sick anymore. No more pain. No more worries. She be with the angels now in heaven." 'Lia buried her face in Adeline's apron. "I wanna go hev'nin with Mama."

**Strangers and Sojourners
in a Town Called Penryn:**

ADELINE

Adeline enfolded the tiny child into her apron and assured her. "One day, my sweet baby, one day our family be all together again in heaven."

Strangers and Sojourners in a Town Called Penryn:

ADELINE

Chapter 13

*I thought about the former days, the years of long ago;
I remembered my song in the night.
My heart mused and my spirit inquired. . .
Psalm 77:5-6*

"'Member, Miss Catheraine, 'member when we was on the prairie? 'Member how you always liked to brush my hair? And you done tol' me the color of my hair reminded you of fresh-brewed coffee? No one done ever tol' me sumptin' like that. You be the first white person to take notice of me as a real person. That be the first time I knew I loved you."

Adeline's soliloquy continued. "Now, here I be, brushing your beautiful soft hair. I am gonna put a silken ribbon around your hair, too. I hope you likes the dress I picked. I knows I not be speaking the way you teached me, but today, it be just me and my ways of talking. Now, your hair all be done up. I gonna wash your face and hands next and put a little pom'granite juice on your lips and cheeks. I always been admiring of how pretty you be and how young

Strangers and Sojourners in a Town Called Penryn:

ADELINE

you always looked—like you be fifteen-years-old instead of twenty-six. . .so young."

Adeline held one of Catheraine's hands, gently washed it, then laid it on the woman's stilled breast. As she lifted the other hand, she brought it to her face, caressing her cheek.

"The first time you touched my cheek was the day Mr. William brought me to your home in Indiana. I thought you was gonna check my teeth, like all them others folks. But it be like you just kissed my face with your soft fingers."

As Adeline remembered more and more tender moments, tears began to roll down her face. She did not brush them away, but allowed them to flow freely. This was her private time to mourn—away from the eyes of those who might not comprehend the grief of a slave girl.

Finished with her tasks, she stepped back from the simple pine coffin. Looking around the room, she spied one last thing that needed to be added. The bird's nest sat on the fireplace mantel. Adeline took the lock of hair out of the nest, her unruly, black, lock of hair, and placed it into

Strangers and Sojourners in a Town Called Penryn:

ADELINE

Catheraine's lifeless hand, curling the stilled woman's fingers around the wavy dark strand.

"I will always be with you—I will always be rememberin' you—I will always be lov'n you, Miss Catheraine."

Strangers and Sojourners in a Town Called Penryn:

ADELINE

Chapter 14

*But I have calmed and quieted my soul,
like a weaned child with its mother;
like a weaned child is my soul within me.
Psalm 131:2*

Catheraine's passing and the ensuing funeral had drained Adeline's energy and strength. William, grief-stricken and bereft of the will to plan his young wife's funeral, leaned on Adeline for encouragement.

The day after the funeral, a weary Adeline was up at her usual time, preparing breakfast for baby Thomas. Mary awoke and came out from her room and joined Adeline at the table.

"Good morning, Miss Mary. You must not be feeling so well, seein' you be up so early."

"I am fine, Adeline. It is just that this second baby is so active that I have a hard time sleeping." Mary paused slightly, then continued. "Also, I need to talk with you about some changes in your duties."

Strangers and Sojourners in a Town Called Penryn:

ADELINE

"Yes'm. I know that two babies might be a handful, but Thomas is becoming quite a helpful little man, so I think we will do just fine."

"Adeline, it's more than just taking care of the babies I am talking about. Adeline." Here Mary paused for quite some time, then continued quickly. "Adeline, this coming Sunday will be your last time for you going to visit at the boarding house."

Adeline's hand, holding baby Thomas' feeding spoon, stopped in mid-air; the oatmeal slowly oozed over the sides of the spoon and finally broke free, plopping onto the table top. Adeline's eyes widened more and more as panic replaced calmness. When she began to speak, the sound of her voice, at first almost a whisper, increased in pitch and timbre, mirroring the panic in her eyes.

"Miss Mary, no, please, no, Miss Mary, please. I will work twice as hard and longer and, oh, please, Miss Mary."

"Adeline,"

Strangers and Sojourners in a Town Called Penryn:

ADELINE

"Please Miss Mary. I gots to see my fam'ly. Please." The spoon dropped to the table as Adeline dropped to her knees, hugging Mary's legs. "They be my fam'ly. Please!"

Mary reached out, hesitantly placing her hand on Adeline's bowed head. Despite the act of kindness shown to Adeline, sternness remained in Mary's voice and words. "I am sorry, Adeline. There is no reason for you to continue with your visits. You will soon understand why. That is my final word on the matter. I will bear no trouble from you." As Mary removed her hand from Adeline's head, Adeline looked up at her owner. The panic in the young girl's eyes receded, replaced with a confused acceptance. "Yes'm. Thank you, Miss Mary. There be no trouble from me." She wiped away her tears, picked up the baby's spoon, refilled it with oatmeal, and finished feeding little Thomas.

Adeline completed the remainder of the week as an automaton; her daily chores so ingrained that they required no conscious effort. She did not cry but neither did she smile. When questioned, she simply answered, "Yes'm" or "No'm," nothing more, nothing less. And for the first time in her life at Stewart's Flat, Sunday came too soon.

Strangers and Sojourners in a Town Called Penryn:

ADELINE

Chapter 15

*For the thing that I fear comes upon me,
and what I dread befalls me.
Job 3:25*

My last day of Sunday visiting. Adeline quietly arose from her pallet, silently dressed in a corner of her room, noiselessly descended the ladder, soundlessly walked passed Thomas' cradle, and stepped out the back door of the house. *My last day of being with my fam'ly.*

Instead of waiting for William to fetch her, Adeline decided to walk the mile to the boarding house, her normal Sunday exuberance replaced with despair.

Mr. William will know what to do. He can talk to Miss Mary. Maybe they can visit with me at the house. T'won't be the same but it be sump'in.

The farther she walked, the lighter her steps became, infused with a hope that her Mr. William would solve the problem. As Adeline rounded the last bend in the road, the front of the boarding house came into her view. She

Strangers and Sojourners in a Town Called Penryn:

ADELINE

spotted William placing 'Lia up on the wagon bench and began running to meet them.

"Mr. William, Mr. William, I be here already!" William did not turn around—did not even acknowledge Adeline. 'Lia held out her arms towards Adeline. As Adeline drew near to the wagon, she could see that 'Lia was crying and calling for her. "Addy! Addy!"

"Shush, honey. I be here! Mr. William, I be here. You can put that wagon away!" William ignored Adeline, settling little the child in the wagon with a gruff, "'Lia, sit down!" This last action was so out-of-character for William that the startled 'Lia halted crying in mid-sob.

"Mr. William, what be the matter? Mr. William? Mr. William!" Adeline practically shouted in the man's face, finally getting his attention.

"Turn around and go back, Adeline!" The harshness in his voice towards her was something new, unexpected. She placed both of her hands on the sides of his face and spoke directly to him.

"Mr. William, I am here. Let's gets inside before Missy catches a cold. We can talk inside."

Strangers and Sojourners in a Town Called Penryn:

ADELINE

"Go home, Adeline."

"No, Mr. William. I want to see 'Lia. We can go inside and talk. We need to talk about my visiting."

"There will no more visiting, Adeline."

"I been told so, Mr. William. But you can think of a way. Talk to Miss Mary and Mr. Joseph. You can think of a way. Please. Let me visit, for 'Lia's sake!"

"After today there will be no reason for you to visit, Adeline. 'Lia will not be here. I am taking her to Sacramento City to a boarding school. The Catholic sisters will take good care of her." William spoke to the air, avoiding Adeline's gaze. His shoulders drooped, his head bowed. "Go home, Adeline."

"NO! NO! NO!" The shy, submissive, yielding Adeline grabbed the horses' harness.

"NO! You cannot take her away from me!" Before William's eyes, the once biddable, compliant, dutiful girl named Adeline transformed into a beseeching, entreating, pleading, weeping girl—fighting for 'Lia as a she-bear might fight for its cubs.

Strangers and Sojourners in a Town Called Penryn:

ADELINE

Chapter 16

*The joy of our hearts has ceased;
our dancing has been turned to mourning.
Lamentations 5:15*

Miss Catheraine--gone to heaven. Annelia, my 'Lia--gone to Sacramento. Mr. William—gone to who-knows-where.

Adeline had not seen William since that doleful Sunday when he had taken 'Lia to the boarding house, nearly two months ago. Although she could no longer visit, she kept a watch out for Mr. William whenever she had a cause to go into town. Today, in preparation for Mary's second child, Mr. Joseph had gone to fetch the mid-wife. At the same time he had dispatched Adeline to Stewart's Flat to check for mail at the postal office. Adeline welcomed any task that allowed her the chance to run into William.

Entering the main road, she took a turn towards the boarding house. The last time Adeline had crossed the threshold of the building was in January, to attend the town-folk's remembering service for Catheraine.

Strangers and Sojourners in a Town Called Penryn:

ADELINE

Now, in March, barely two months later, she approached its entrance with a different purpose—to find out anything she could about Mr. William's whereabouts. The bell attached to the doorjamb jingled as Adeline pushed open the front door. Once inside the entryway parlor she spotted Mrs. Verholtz, the proprietor, coming down the stairwell in answer to the bell's ringing.

"Hello, Miz Verholtz."

The landlady peered over the railing while continuing down the staircase, surprise and curiosity in her voice. "Well, Adeline. What brings you here?"

"Miz Verholtz, I be, I mean, I am wondering if you seen Mr. William lately."

"I'm sorry, Adeline, but William moved out of here after he took 'Lia to the orphanage."

Adeline looked warily at the woman. "Orphanage? Ain't you mean boarding school?"

Mrs. Verholtz backtracked a little. "Um, yes. Well, it is a boarding school and an orphanage also. Most of the children, like Annelia, have lost only one parent. So in a sense, they're not really orphans but are placed there to get

Strangers and Sojourners in a Town Called Penryn:

ADELINE

an education while the remaining parent works. Don't you worry none, Adeline. 'Lia will be well taken care of. And I'm sure that your Mr. William will visit her as often as he is able."

Crestfallen, Adeline could only reply, "Yes'm. I'm sure she be fine."

Silence stood between the two, daring one or the other to break the stillness. Adeline, determined to fulfill her mission at the boarding house, interrupted the quietude with a hushed inquiry.

"Miz Verholtz, might you know where Mr. William be staying?" Her eyes implored the busy woman for just a little bit of information. The older woman hesitated, sighed, then convinced herself to share her knowledge with Adeline.

"Well, I think he might be staying in the office at his mining operation, at least that's what I overheard from one of my boarders." Seeing Adeline's solemn eagerness to find William, she knelt down to be at eye-level with Addie and took ahold of the young girl's hands. "If I happen to see William in town, I will tell him you were asking for him."

Strangers and Sojourners in a Town Called Penryn:

ADELINE

The almost twelve-year-old Adeline nodded her head. "Thank you, ma'am. Thank you."

Adeline's spirits lifted a bit at the news of William's whereabouts. *Now, I jes' needs to find a reason to visit Mr. William at his office.*

Strangers and Sojourners in a Town Called Penryn:

ADELINE

Chapter 17

*Love bears all things, believes all things,
hopes all things, endures all things.
I Corinthians 13:7*

Mary Ella Goldstan made her appearance at Stewart's Flat on a cold, blustery day in March 1856. Three-year-old Thomas greeted his sister with a shriek of disdain at this new intrusion into his formerly solitary world. Adeline hugged the young boy, comforting him and shushing him at the same time. "Ain't you worry, Master Thomas. You being the oldest chile' makes you real impor'ant. It is your job, now, to watch after little Mary Ella and help keep her safe. You are the big brother!"

Thomas gazed up at Adeline. "Really? I'm 'portent?" His three-year-old chest filled with pride at his new station in life.

"Really, Master Thomas. Really."

A week later, an unexpected visitor knocked on the front door of the Goldstan residence.

Strangers and Sojourners in a Town Called Penryn:

ADELINE

Adeline had just finished helping Thomas eat his breakfast while Mary sat by the fire watching tiny Ella sleep in the rocking cradle. (Joseph and Mary had decided to use "Ella," the baby's middle name, to prevent any confusion between the two Marys.) The visitor knocked again, slightly harder. Mary started rocking the cradle so that Ella wouldn't wake up.

"Adeline, will you hurry-up and get the front door."

"Yes'm." She opened the front door, about to welcome in the guest, but was unable to move. She stood, entranced, for so long and so silently that Mary finally called out, "For goodness' sake, Adeline, allow Mr. Barton in and close the door before all the heat escapes!"

William half-smiled at Adeline as he crossed the threshold. He removed his hat and scarf, the scarf that Adeline had made for him, and handed them to the still unspeaking girl. "Be sure and take care of that woolen muffler. It means a lot to me." He smiled, a full smile, and gave a wink to Adeline.

Adeline came to life. "Oh, Mr. William! Mr. William!" She hugged William so long that he had to break

Strangers and Sojourners in a Town Called Penryn:

ADELINE

her hold on him. Mary brought Adeline back to her proper place and role.

"Adeline, please hang up Mr. Barton's things by the fire. Then you may fetch him a cup of coffee. After that, please dress Thomas and take him outside for a walk."

"Yes'm." She filled a cup with coffee, handed it to William, then turned and picked up Thomas. As she walked to the bedroom, she glanced back at Mary and William. Neither said a word to her as she continued past.

Outside, Thomas explored the rocks and crevices, looking for lizards. Ordinarily, Adeline loved this part of the day, walking with young Thomas, uncovering sleeping blue-belly lizards, discovering the slinky critters' hiding places. Ordinarily, she had a hard time returning to the house and her inside chores. Ordinarily. But, today was not ordinary. She hurried Thomas along, anxious to return to the house, afraid that Mr. William would leave before she had a chance to talk with him.

Thomas, finally bored with his adventure, took off running towards the house. "Cain't catch me! Cain't catch me!" Normally, Adeline pursued him, but never caught

Strangers and Sojourners in a Town Called Penryn:

ADELINE

him, a part of the game they played. Today, however, she caught up and surpassed him, putting the toddler into a foul mood. "No fair! I'm s'posed to win!" He plopped to the ground, crossed his arms, and scowled up at Adeline.

"Come on, Thomas, it is time for rest."

"Not gonna rest!"

"Yes, Thomas, you are gonna rest. Now, please get yo'self on up."

"Not gonna!"

In an uncharacteristic move, Adeline scooped up the pouting child and carried him under her arm like a sack of potatoes. Thomas, shocked at this here-to-fore unknown treatment, flailed his arms and legs. "Put me down—put me down—I'll tell mama!" Adeline, surprised at what she had just done, set Thomas down on the ground. "I am sorry, Master Thomas. But I need to talk to Mr. William before he leaves. How about I give you sump'in sweet before you take your rest? Will you come along then?"

"A molasses cookie?" He thought a little longer and held up his fingers. "Two cookies?"

"Hmm. Yes. Two cookies for you!"

Strangers and Sojourners in a Town Called Penryn:

ADELINE

"Goody! You can win ev'ry time if you give me two cookies!"

As they approached the house, Adeline saw William's horse still tethered to the fence post. She guided Thomas through the back door entrance to his bedroom, fetched the cookies, and milk, watched while Thomas ate his reward, tucked him into bed, quietly walked out the back door, then waited for William by his horse. In a short while, William came out the front door. As he came near to his horse, Adeline approached him from the other side.

"There you are, Addie. I was hoping to get to speak with you before I left." Adeline started to reply, but William held up his hand to stop her. "Let me say what I need to say, Addie." He neared her, gently placing His hand on her sloping shoulder. "I am sorry for how I treated you the last time we saw each other. I am sorry that circumstances have torn our family apart. I am sorry that I had to take Annelia away from you. I never meant to hurt you or 'Lia, yet it seems that I have wounded you both. I only pray that you both will be able to forgive me. . .that someday you both will realize that I had no choice to do what I did.

Strangers and Sojourners in a Town Called Penryn:

ADELINE

That I was only thinking of doing what I thought was best for both of you. Can you understand? Can you forgive me?"

"Mr. William, you done pained me, but I will mend. I know that you were hurting awful bad. We all loved Miss Catheraine and we all miss her sump'in fierce. I only wisht that 'Lia could have stayed with me. I forgive you, Mr. William. We are fam'ly. Fam'ly forgives."

William knelt down, enveloped Adeline in his arms, and whispered, "Thank you."

Adeline, overwhelmed with grace, simply affirmed, "Welcome home, Mr. William."

From that day on, William made every effort to visit Adeline at least once a month. Adeline relished the impromptu visits and Miss Mary allowed the unscheduled stopovers as long as Adeline wasn't needed at the moment.

During those times, William would share stories about his visits with 'Lia, how she was doing in school, and how the Sisters of Mercy had taken a special interest in her,

Strangers and Sojourners in a Town Called Penryn:

ADELINE

spoiling her beyond what might have been appropriate and for her own good.

"Of course," he heartily related, "Annelia knows how to get what she wants but always in a way that doesn't make her look self-indulgent. In fact, her good-standing with the nuns enable her to help other classmates who don't have such a good relationship with the sisters. Because of her wit and generosity, she is well-loved by teachers and peers alike. The few reproaches that they have regarding 'Lia—namely her acerbic manner of speaking and her somewhat defiant nature—are offset by the child's heartfelt desire to be accepted by others."

Adeline pictured the young girl petitioning the nuns on behalf of her schoolmates; the twinkle in the child's eye that was so hard to resist.

"When will you bring her back for a visit, Mr. William?"

"When she is older and can stay at the boarding house during the summer, Adeline. Just a while longer."

Every March, of each successive year, Adeline asked the same question. "This year, Mr. William?"

**Strangers and Sojourners
in a Town Called Penryn:**

ADELINE

Every March, the same answer. "Just a while longer, Adeline."

Susan Mary Goldstan entered the world in the spring of 1859, joining her two siblings, six-year-old Thomas and three-year-old Mary Ella. Annelia celebrated her seventh birthday at the orphanage while fourteen-year-old Adeline celebrated alone and waited for the day of 'Lia's return to Stewart's Flat.

**Strangers and Sojourners
in a Town Called Penryn:**

ADELINE

Chapter 18

*The Lord foils the plans of the nations;
he thwarts the purposes of the peoples.
But the plans of the Lord stand forever,
the purposes of his heart through all generations.
Psalm 33:10-11*

1864

The days, weeks, months, and years carried on. Adeline once overheard Joseph say, "Time and tide wait for no man," and realized the truth in the saying. All around her people were changing, growing up, moving away, getting married, and passing on. Even countries were changing, according to all those town-folks concerned about the Civil War. Mr. Joseph wanted to go back to Mississippi and "fight them know-it-all northerners," but Miss Mary had implored him to stay in California, especially since she was with child again.

Though their faces had become as a faded rose to her and their names long forgotten, Adeline prayed daily

Strangers and Sojourners in a Town Called Penryn:

ADELINE

for the slaves on the plantation, thankful that providence had scurried her away from the destruction visited upon the southern states. She listened intently as Mr. Joseph read the latest letter from home, listing the account of deaths of friends and family members. Among them, Kay Stewart of Lafayette, Mississippi—the co-founder of Stewart's Flat, California. When the town residents received the news of his death, everyone gathered for a memorial service to honor his memory.

Adeline also noticed a change in the gold workers as she carried out her chores in town. Many of the mines were now closed as the excavations for new gold deposits grew harder and more dangerous, causing many of the owners and workers to turn their energies to the age-old occupation of farming and raising livestock. Adeline saw them at the mercantile, exchanging their pickaxes for plows. As she watched the transformation of industry take place in her town, she marveled at the adaptability of so many men, women, and families. Even Mary and Joseph had decided to sell the Goldstan mining interests and search for farmland around Stewart's Flat.

Strangers and Sojourners in a Town Called Penryn:

ADELINE

Then came the rumors of the welshman. The gossip ran all through the town and Adeline heard all about in every store that she entered.

"His name is Griffith Griffith. Yes, both names are the same. Says he wants to buy land but not farmland and not gold-bearing land."

"He wants to start a business. Says that we got good rock around here."

A bystander scoffed. "Good rock? What good are rocks if it ain't got gold?"

"Listen here. He's a stonecutter, a quarryman from overseas; a place called Wales where they know a thing or two about rock mining. This man says our granite is as fine a rock as he's ever seen back home. Says its quality is superior for buildings and such. And with the Central Pacific Railroad Line coming so close to town, he wants to set up a quarry just up the road from Stewart's Flat. And here's the best part. He says that there will be plenty of jobs for us out-of-work gold-miners!"

Enthused by the prospect of work and industry, many townsmen welcomed the peculiarly accented welsh-

**Strangers and Sojourners
in a Town Called Penryn:**

ADELINE

man with open arms, anxious to being earning a living by any means other than farming.

***

Joseph, now free from his mining interests, put all of his energies into establishing a viable farming business. His somewhat casual search for land increased in urgency as his family increased in number. Joseph Francis joined his family in the early months of 1864. Brown-haired, brown-eyed, brown-skinned Thomas was now eleven; fair-haired, Mary Ella, eight; Susan Mary, five.

All the while, the now nineteen-year-old Adeline dutifully cared for the children and patiently waited for the time that "little" 'Lia would turn twelve—old enough to come back and live at Stewart's Flat during the summer months.

Strangers and Sojourners in a Town Called Penryn:

ADELINE

Chapter 19

Above all, keep fervent in your love for one another, because love covers a multitude of sins.
I Peter 4:8

Goldstan Residence
May 1864

I am about as jittery as a milk-pail hanging on a covered wagon. Adeline, sitting on the back door step, kept tap, tap, tapping her foot on the dusty ground. *No reason for me to be so twitchy, it just be my sweet 'Lia coming home for a visit.* Tappity, tappity, tappity. *I hope she remembers me--I cain't believe it been **eight** years since I last seen her.* She arose from the stoop and began pacing the width of the house, stopping abruptly at the sound of a wagon making its way up the road. With the palms of her hands, she smoothed the wrinkles out the front of her apron, returned an unruly strand of hair back under her Sunday hat, picked up the straw basket full of freshly picked wildflowers that rested on the step, and turned to

Strangers and Sojourners in a Town Called Penryn:

ADELINE

face the approaching wagon. Now, instead of fidgeting, she resembled Lot's wife after the fall of Sodom and Gomorrah—a rigid human pillar fashioned out of a block of salt, unable to proceed any further.

William *whoa-ed* the team of horses, jumped down, crossed to the other side of the wagon, and helped his daughter alight. Still, Adeline did not move. The "child" that she was expecting, the once chubby, tousled-haired, rambunctious, messy toddler no longer existed; rather, in her place stood a refined, genteel, exceedingly mature-looking (i.e., twelve-year-old who looks twenty) maiden. 'Lia nodded at Adeline, but did not make a move towards her. Adeline, rooted to the spot, continued to survey the girl from top to bottom. The eight year separation had played a cruel trick on Adeline, deceiving her recollection. She had not witnessed the gradual transformation of 'Lia like she had with the Goldstan children. An aloof stranger stood before her. A stylish, cultivated, and obviously wealthy member of society. The type of person a black servant had been taught not to inconvenience. Adeline's upbringing dictated,

Strangers and Sojourners in a Town Called Penryn:

ADELINE

"She is superior to you. Keep your distance," while her heart whispered, *"She is Catheraine's child. Go to her."*

William slowly approached Adeline. Taking her hand, he guided her to 'Lia.

"'Lia, this is Adeline, your mama's earthly angel, the one I told you about each time I visited with you."

'Lia rolled her eyes, flaunting her pre-teen attitude and disdain at his statement. "I know who she is, Father. I am not daft." After this slight, she turned to Adeline. "Hello, Addie. It is delightful to see that you are in good health. To be owned, uh, pardon me, to be **kept** by such a fine family as the Goldstans has worked well in your favor."

Astonished at 'Lia's bold and hurtful statement, Adeline could only reply as a dutiful inferior. "Yes'm."

William, agitated and embarrassed by his daughter's demeanor and rudeness, grabbed her arm. "'ANNELIA! Apologize to Addie at once."

Feigning contrition, 'Lia placed her hands on Adeline's shoulders. "My dear Addie, I am *so* sorry for mentioning your station in life. Please forgive me." She turned back around, faced her father, and impudently asked,

Strangers and Sojourners in a Town Called Penryn:

ADELINE

"There, Fah—ther. Are you satisfied?" With this last remark hanging in the air, she flounced back towards the wagon, climbed aboard, and waited for William to take her to the boarding house.

William placed his arm around Adeline's shoulder as if to shield her from the hurtful words.

"I am truly sorry, Adeline, for my mollycoddled child. I know she harbors resentment towards me for handing her over to the Sisters. I didn't realize that her hostility spilled over onto you as well. She never let on that she harbored ill feelings towards you. I have a lot to make up to her. Please forgive her, Addie. Though she may well look to be nearly grown, it seems that inside she is just a young temperamental child trying to understand why she was abandoned by all who loved her." Unhappiness overwhelmed William.

Adeline clasped William's hands. "It be okay, Mr. William. It be okay."

William could not see 'Lia at that moment. Only Adeline witnessed the solitary teardrop that trickled down

Strangers and Sojourners in a Town Called Penryn:

ADELINE

the young girl's cheek, lingering there until the air dried away its existence.

The ride to the boarding house was conducted in silence. William, trying hard to control his distaste at 'Lia's exchange with Adeline, decided it would be best not speak at the moment. 'Lia, aware of her father's disapproval and disappointment at her actions, stared straight ahead. Adeline sat behind the two, the welcoming basket of flowers resting on her lap, and mulled over how to bridge the silence between father and daughter.

As the boarding house came into view, William finally broke the silence. "Annelia, you will not be rooming alone. I have hired a Mrs. Barnes, a widow, to be your chaperone and roommate. I hope that you will be more courteous to her than you were with Adeline."

"Yes, Father."

William stopped the wagon and turned to face his daughter. "In regards to Adeline, you will treat her with respect. She has been a part of our family since you were one-year old. She helped your mama raise you. She took

Strangers and Sojourners in a Town Called Penryn:

ADELINE

care of your mama through her sickness. You may not remember all the kindness and love that she gave to you, but that does not give you the right to demean her based solely on her race and position in life. She has waited for eight years to have you back in her life. You will visit with her and your visits will be gracious and mannerly. If you have learned anything at your school, you have learned how to comport yourself in a social setting. Please put into practice what the Sisters have taught." The gentle scolding over, 'Lia reached for William's hand, held it between her own two small hands, and humbly acquiesced with a quiet, "Yes, Papa."

'Lia then turned to Adeline. Offered her hand to the quiet servant and meekly declared, "Adeline, I look forward to visiting with you this summer."

Annelia's appointed chaperone and guardian greeted William and 'Lia in the foyer of the boarding house.

"Mrs. Barnes, " William spoke as he guided his daughter forward, "this is Annelia, my daughter. Annelia, this is Mrs. Rhoda Barnes."

Strangers and Sojourners in a Town Called Penryn:

ADELINE

Both females surveyed each other as they shook hands. Adeline stood back, observing the stilted interactions between the caretaker and her young pre-teen charge.

"Hello, Mrs. Barnes. I am pleased to meet you."

"Thank you, Miss Annelia. I am looking forward to our summer together."

"Yes, ma'am." Annelia tried to contain her surprise at meeting her "adult" caretaker, but a smile gave away her slight astonishment. Adeline, too, smiled at the appointed caretaker. She had imagined that the keeper would be an older woman with gray hair and maybe a slightly stooped back. Instead, a young, barely twenty-five- year-old, extremely plain-faced woman stood rigidly before Annelia. Her slick-backed hair, fashioned in a bun at the nape of her neck, along with the plain black skirt and and high-necked starched white shirt, gave her an air of unquestioned authority. As William and Mrs. Barnes stood side-by-side, waiting for 'Lia to continue, Annelia noted that Mrs. Barnes' height nearly equaled William's.

"Come, Annelia. Cat got your tongue?" William grinned as he broke his daughter's and Adeline's reveries.

Strangers and Sojourners in a Town Called Penryn:

ADELINE

"What? Oh, yes, Papa. I guess I was lost in my thoughts. My apologies, Mrs. Barnes."

"Apology accepted Miss. I suppose you expected someone a little older. Let me assure you, though, that my age does not keep me from fulfilling my duties. As long as you are in my care you will adhere to the rules of decency required of young ladies. Your father and I have formed a list of acceptable activities in which you may participate. We can go over these tomorrow. Right now, let's take your things to our room and get you settled in."

Adeline discerned that Mrs. Barnes took an instant liking to 'Lia. The widow marveled at the twelve-year-old girl's quick wit, melodious laugh, and educational knowledge. As the summer progressed, the two formed a bond of friendship more like sisters rather than that of caretaker and charge; Mrs. Barnes being the older sister, domineering and motherly; Annelia, the younger sibling, spunky and rebellious.

Adeline's and 'Lia's interactions, at first constrained and awkward, developed into a less formal manner as each became accustomed to the other's mannerisms and mus-

Strangers and Sojourners in a Town Called Penryn:

ADELINE

ings. But while 'Lia and Mrs. Barnes became fast friends, 'Lia's still retained a suppressed air of superiority over Adeline.

Mrs. Barnes and Annelia visited with Addie at the Gooslby home twice a week. Mary, upon William's request, reinstated Adeline's Sunday day off while Annelia was staying in town.

When Adeline happened to be invited to join in on one of their adventures, 'Lia treated her with a courteous regard but the closeness and fondness that had once been between the child and servant girl did not carryover with the almost-grown 'Lia. Mrs. Barnes, too, was pleasant towards Adeline, but not like Catheraine had been. Adeline, recognizing that what was lost might never again be regained, still relished each moment spent with 'Lia.

Early each Sunday morning, Adeline happily walked to the boarding house then waited in the dining room for her family. William would arrive a few minutes later. Together they would talk about the past week's visits

Strangers and Sojourners in a Town Called Penryn:

ADELINE

while waiting for the last members of the Sunday group to awake and join them for breakfast.

The summer of 1864 passed all too quickly for Adeline. Now, on the last Sunday of the season, the last day of Annelia's summer at Stewart's Flat, Adeline sat at the boarding house dining table. William sat across from her, both waiting for the young girl-woman to join them. This day, while waiting, they chatted about the entire summer of comings-and-goings of 'Lia and Mrs. Barnes: picnics, wagon rides, church socials, and the town's Fourth of July celebration.

"Here comes the sleepy head!" Annelia announced as she hurried down the stairwell. Mrs. Barnes, Annelia's "alarm clock", followed behind the girl, her straight posture and slow-measured gait in direct contrast to her young charge's energetic leaps and bounds.

Annelia hugged her father's neck then kissed him on his forehead. "Good morning, Papa." Plopping down in the chair beside her father, she glanced over at Adeline. "Good morning, Adeline."

Strangers and Sojourners in a Town Called Penryn:

ADELINE

"Good morning, Missy 'Lia. Good morning, Miss Rhoda."

Arriving last to the table, the widow Barnes nodded at Adeline then William. "Good morning, Mr. Barton." William motioned for 'Lia's chaperone to take the chair next to his. 'Lia and Adeline both covertly raised their eyebrows at this seemingly innocent act of manners. Nothing was said between the two about what had just occurred, but the image stuck in each one's mind, giving rise to speculation about the relationship between 37-year-old William, the widower father, and 25-year-old Rhoda, the widow chaperone.

The foursome breakfasted, chattered, laughed, quieted, then tearfully said their goodbyes. 'Lia returned to her far-off orphanage, Rhoda returned to her single room, William returned to his gold mining office, and Adeline returned to her rightful place.

***

Annelia's, Rhoda's and Adeline's next summer together, the summer of 1865, mirrored the previous year. Adeline once again looked forward to Sunday visits with

Strangers and Sojourners in a Town Called Penryn:

ADELINE

Mr. William and 'Lia. She silently observed 'Lia's ways and how her manners had evolved since the previous year. 'Lia was now quite a polished young lady; a very pretty one at that. And Adeline wasn't the only one who noticed. Boys' heads turned in her direction as she walked down the street. She would smile politely at the admirers, causing the blood to rush to the awkward youths' faces. Rhoda and Adeline chuckled at their reactions.

With each year's passing, the young girl's premature comeliness blossomed into full-fledged beauty. During the summer of 1866, William and Mrs. Barnes bandied suitor requests like a badminton shuttlecock. Neither considered fourteen-year-old Annelia old enough to be courted, but the persistent young men kept on calling. William, Rhoda, and Adeline hovered over 'Lia throughout the summer, thankful that she would be back in Sacramento City under the watchful eyes of the nuns by the fall season.

Strangers and Sojourners in a Town Called Penryn:

ADELINE

Chapter 20

*In the day of prosperity be joyful,
and in the day of adversity consider:
God has made the one as well as the other, . . .
Ecclesiastes 7:14*

**1867
Goldstan Residence**

Adeline observed from the doorway stoop as Mary and Joseph announced to their brood that the Goldstan household would be moving. They had kept this secret from their children for two years so as to spare themselves the, "When is the house going to finished?" litany.

Fourteen-year-old Thomas, eleven-year-old Ella, eight-year-old Susan and even three-year-old Joseph Jr. (lovingly called Frankie) ran wildly through their too tiny house, overturning chairs in the process.

The children hooted and hollered so loudly that Adeline finally had to shush them all—her own unenthusiastic feelings about the move stood in stark opposition to the children's jubilation. To the youngsters, a new house

Strangers and Sojourners in a Town Called Penryn:

ADELINE

signaled new adventures in uncharted and unexplored territory. To Adeline, the move meant more distance between her, Mr. William, and 'Lia. She silently shushed herself, warding off the impending loneliness she feared to come.

The farm be only about three miles west from Stewart's Flat, part of that new town of Pino. It not be far too far away.

But she knew that this necessary move signaled the end of her impromptu walks into town. No longer a chance of accidentally running into Mr. William or 'Lia while dutifully picking up supplies at the store. No longer the opportunity to place flowers on Miss Catheraine's grave after completing her errands.

Little Frankie tugged at Adeline's skirt, bringing the preoccupied nanny's attention back to the surrounding rumpus. Scooping up the child into her arms, Adeline put her own low spirits aside and joined in the hoopla with the children. *God, He been good to me. He knows how I feel. God knows. No need for me to be a-worrying.* Joseph's booming voice broke through her reverie.

Strangers and Sojourners in a Town Called Penryn:

ADELINE

"Okay, all you children. Let's get on that wagon and go see your new home!"

***

"Mr. William." No response. "Mr. William, we gots to talk." Still no response. Adeline continued on through the silence. "Okay then, you gots to listen." William turned to Adeline, raising an eyebrow at her abruptness towards him. Adeline inhaled deeply then plunged forward.

"Mr. William, 'Lia don't want to go back to school after this summer. She don't tell me this, but I know. I over heared her confiding to Mr. Leonard Lawson. She don't want to go back. She wants to live here in Stewart's Flat." Gasping for air, Adeline continued. "Let her stay here, Mr. William. She be old enough, now. Miss Rhoda loves 'Lia like a daughter, she done tol' me. And I know'd 'Lia would be happy to live with her. And. . .and she will be closer to me."

Silence. William stared straight ahead through the mining office building's lone window, his line of sight focused on the far horizon.

Strangers and Sojourners in a Town Called Penryn:

ADELINE

With a tentative touch, Adeline took hold of William's hand and softly implored, "Mr. William. Let her come home to you—to me. Maybe this be our chance to be a fam'ly again."

William's gaze never wavered from the window. Adeline's gaze never wavered from William's face.

The distant hammering of the stamp mill resounded through the office, invading the silence.

"All right, Adeline, you win. 'Lia can stay. But I will inform her at my own time and in my own way. In no way are you to speak with her about this. Agreed?"

Adeline's heart swelled with gratitude and filled with the renewed hope of being a part of a real family again. "Yes sir, Mr. William. I promise not to say one word."

Each time Adeline visited with 'Lia and the widow Barnes, it was with the expectation of 'Lia's announcement of staying in Stewart's Flat. Adeline, determined to keep her promise to William, uttered not a word on the subject. Even when 'Lia would whine and complain about returning to the boarding school in the fall, Adeline held her tongue. *After*

Strangers and Sojourners in a Town Called Penryn:

ADELINE

all, she reasoned to herself, *it be Mr. William's place to speak of such matters to his daughter.*

The end of June of 1867 neared. Still, William had not spoken to 'Lia about remaining in town instead of returning to school in Sacramento City.

Adeline, on an errand from Mary, drove the work cart purposefully into town. Along the way, she constantly scanned the road, hoping to have a chance encounter with William. She needed to broach the subject of 'Lia's staying in Stewart's Flat. Providence was with her. Mr. William stood on the porch of the hotel/boarding house, hands in his pockets, chewing on a toothpick, shifting the sharpened sliver of wood back and forth with his lips. Adeline encouraged the horse to move a bit faster, cracking the leather whip just above the critter's right ear.

"Mr. William." Adeline alit from the cart and tied the reins to the front post. "Mr. William, 'Lia is still fretting about returnin' to school in September. I be thinkin' it may be time for you to tell her the news of her stayin'."

William nodded in agreement to the suggestion. "The time is almost here, Adeline, to tell her the news."

Strangers and Sojourners
in a Town Called Penryn:

ADELINE

"Hmm. Please don't mind my askin', but, when be that time, Mr. William?"

William, with a twinkle in his eye and a sly smile on his lips, took Adeline's hand. "Come, I'll *show* you when the time will be right." He led her to his work wagon, helped her up to the driver's seat, climbed in beside her, and gave the horse team a gentle slap with the reins.

William steered the wagon northward, away from the town, back the way Adeline had just come. The team plodded slowly up the steep hill, past the Alabama Mine. As they continued on the slope and around the many bends in the road, they couldn't help but notice the latest mining enterprise forming on the outskirts of town.

"Mercy. Looks like that Mr. Griffith 'bout be ready to start his granite business. I just don't figure how digging up rocks can make someone a decent living. What do you think, Mr. William?"

"I think that Mr. Griffith is smarter than all of us gold-diggers combined. And, I think I just might ask him for a job."

Strangers and Sojourners in a Town Called Penryn:

ADELINE

"A job? What'chu need a job for? You got the 'Lizbeth Mine to keep you in gold for a lifetime. Hmphh."

"Well, Adeline, I am getting just a little too old to be working a mine and who knows how much gold is left to get. The mine has provided me with enough funds to carry me through many more years. And I miss my old profession, wagon building and blacksmithing. I sold my mine last week. The new owner will be taking over in a month."

Adeline nodded. "Well, I knowed Mr. Joseph wanted to try farming again. But I never accounted the reason as being that the gold might almost be gone. I jes' thought with the children gettin' so big and their ole house be gettin' so small that the fam'ly needed to move."

William prompted the wagon team to move a little faster. As the two traveled, they chatted just like they had on the California Trail, fourteen years earlier. William the redeemer, Adeline the redeemed.

William slowed the horses with a gentle tug of the reins and a soft, "Whoa, there."

Adeline, so consumed with talking with her "Mr. William," failed to notice the unfinished house that now

Strangers and Sojourners
in a Town Called Penryn:

ADELINE

arose before her. William turned the young woman's head toward the modest structure.

"Addie, when this is completed, that's when I'll tell 'Lia she can stay. I wanted to give her a real home, not another boarding house."

A simple, white, one-and-a-half story clapboard home rested upon a granite block foundation. Scrub oaks, buck-eye trees, and gangly weeds landscaped the area around the new dwelling.

"Oh, Mr. William, it be beautiful!" Adeline walked the perimeter of the small house. William trailed behind her.

At the back of the home, granite steps led down to the cold cellar basement. Above the basement opening, acting as a door stoop, William had placed an outside (but enclosed) stairwell to the attic bedroom.

"I wanted 'Lia to feel as if she had her own little house, so I made the door to her room accessible from the outside. It's not a big house, nor a grand one, but it is a house. I only wish. . ."

Strangers and Sojourners in a Town Called Penryn:

ADELINE

His voice faded, the remaining words lost to Adeline. But she knew.

"I wished it, too, Mr. William. Miss Catheraine would be right pleased with this home."

A 12 x 16 living area with a corner fireplace, two 8 x 8 bedrooms off of the living room, and a step-down 8 x 16 kitchen-eating room lean-to attached to the other side of the living area completed the house layout.

Adeline closed her eyes, envisioning a furnished home.

When she opened her eyes, she caught William watching her closely.

"Well, do you think she will like it?"

"Oh, Mr. William, it be perfect. How much longer until she can come home?"

"It will be finished in two weeks, the same time I hand over my business. I want to have everything in place when she comes. Mrs. Barnes is helping me to make sure all is in order. She is just as excited as I am to have 'Lia come to live here. I believe she loves 'Lia just as much as

Strangers and Sojourners in a Town Called Penryn:

ADELINE

we do, Adeline. Just think, this will be a new start for all of us."

As the interminable two weeks passed, Adeline worried over 'Lia's apparent unhappiness, visible to all who spent any time with the teenaged girl. Although she had promised William to remain silent, there were many times she came close to breaking her vow—practically each time she visited with the sullen fifteen-year-old.

Adeline did notice one exception to 'Lia's depressing mood swings. When Mr. Lawson came a calling, 'Lia's spirits perked right up. Her sighing and listlessness gone at the sound of Leonard's knock on the door followed by his hearty "Hello in there".

Adeline positioned herself near 'Lia each time she entertained the handsome, older, family friend. *He may be a special to the fam'ly, but I still gots my res'vations 'bout his intentions. 'Lia be too pretty to be jes' a family friend.* However, since the downhearted girl's spirits lifted each time he came calling, her youthful exuberance replaced

**Strangers and Sojourners
in a Town Called Penryn:**

ADELINE

with an adult-like social grace, Adeline refrained from voicing her concerns about their friendship.

Visiting days followed a familiar pattern. 'Lia sat by the front window of the boarding house parlor, pouting about being bored. Mrs. Barnes sat next to her and worked on a needlepoint pillow cover. Adeline tried to dispel the gloominess by recounting the family's crossing of the Great Plains, the long days of travel, the short nights of sleep. Her endless chatter aimed at lifting the young 'Lia's dark mood.

"Your mama, she be so brave to leave everything behind and travel with you, and you being barely jus' one-year old. Plus, she had to teach me about takin' care of babies at the same time. She was sumpt'in special." No response from Annelia to Adeline's prompt.

A hush fell over the room. Adeline lowered her head, remembering the kindness and love bestowed upon her by 'Lia's mother. She longed for Catheraine's gentle words of encouragement and warm embraces freely given to a plain servant girl. Looking up, she noticed 'Lia staring intently at her. Adeline averted her eyes for second then looked back at 'Lia. The young girl's bitter scrutiny re-

Strangers and Sojourners in a Town Called Penryn:

ADELINE

mained focused on a bewildered Adeline. *Why you be disliken me so much? Why?*

Wistfully, Adeline continued. "I loved your mama, Missy 'Lia. She was the kindest person on this earth. She showed love to this ole' darkie and showed me how to love others."

'Lia turned away from Adeline, the rebuff so deliberate that even Mrs. Barnes appeared flustered at the girl's outward sign of disdain.

A knock at the door followed by the expected "Hello in there" dissipated the uneasiness that had surfaced in the room.

"He sure be early enough today. Sun's barely been up for an hour." With a sigh, Adeline arose to receive Mr. Leonard. She half-smiled at 'Lia as the girl-woman hurriedly smoothed out her cotton dress, pinched some color into her cheeks, and arranged a stray strand of hair—all before coming face-to-face with her proclaimed best *friend*.

'Lia and Leonard carried on like long-lost chums, catching up on time gone by.

Strangers and Sojourners in a Town Called Penryn:

ADELINE

Humph, they just saw each other last week. Don't know what all the fuss is about. Adeline muttered to herself, kept a close eye on the two friends, and continued mending socks all the while. *Maybe Mr. William should rethink about sending her back to school being she only fifteen-year. More schoolin' might be best for her, leastways better than entertaining all them other young bucks that wanna be suitors. Mr. Leonard ain't gonna be the only friendly feller to come-a-callin' on Missy. And those others ain't gonna be settlin' to be jes' friends.*

"Excuse me, Mrs. Barnes," 'Lia's speaking broke through Adeline's thoughts. "Mr. Lawson would like to escort me to the mine to see father."

Adeline began gathering her sewing. "That be fine, Missy. I be ready to join you in a few minutes."

"I was speaking to Mrs. Barnes, Adeline. After all, she is my official caretaker."

"Yes'm Miss 'Lia. I meant no disrespect. I just be getting my things to take with me when we go." Chagrined, Adeline sheepishly looked to the widow Barnes then to

Strangers and Sojourners in a Town Called Penryn:

ADELINE

Leonard Lawson who silently raised his eyebrows at 'Lia, wordlessly admonishing her to mind her manners.

'Lia deferred to his chastening, taming the pertness in her voice. "Pardon me, Adeline. It's just that Mrs. Barnes has the final say so in my comings and goings."

"Request granted, my dear." Mrs. Barnes continued. "I could accompany you if you prefer."

'Lia glanced around the room, bit her lower lip, avoiding eye contact with Adeline and Mrs. Barnes.

"Um, well, what I would really like to ask is, um. . .well, can Leonard, I mean, Mr. Lawson, escort me without a chaperone? Papa's office is not too far from here. And you know that Papa trusts Mr. Lawson with my well-being. After all, it's not like he's an irresponsible school boy. Leonard is a very respectable twenty-six-year-old business man, old enough to be my. . . my . . .brother." A slight smile formed on Leonard's face at hearing 'Lia describe him as a brother figure.

Adeline looked to Mrs. Barnes. Mrs. Barnes raised her eyebrows at Adeline, signaling her uncertainty of the

Strangers and Sojourners in a Town Called Penryn:

ADELINE

request. Adeline answered back with a questioning nod of her head.

An internal battle warred within Adeline. *What harm can come? The mine is just a mile away and lots of people be walking that way. 'Sides, Mr. Leonard be a true family friend. He will take good care of 'Lia, him being so much older and protective of her.*

The two chaperones nodded at each other then at 'Lia.

"Be back by lunch time, no later," demanded Mrs. Barnes. " And 'Lia, I will get a full report from your father as to when you arrived and departed. If I discern any improprieties, this will be the last time you will be alone with Mr. Lawson. Understood?"

'Lia ran to the widow, threw her arms around the woman's neck, and kissed her cheek. "Oh, thank you, dearest Rhoda! Thank you so much." Passing by Adeline, she grabbed Leonard's hand, pulled him towards the door, and winked at him. "Come on, L*eona*--I mean, Mr. Lawson. Don't dawdle. Time is a-wasting!" With one last glance towards Rhoda and Adeline, 'Lia hurried out the door, waving

Strangers and Sojourners
in a Town Called Penryn:

ADELINE

good-bye as she crossed the threshold. Stepping up into the buggy, she pushed aside a valise that rested on the floorboard. Adeline, caught up in 'Lia's enthusiasm, never once considered the significance of that satchel in the buggy.

Lunchtime came and went without the company of 'Lia and Leonard. Adeline worried that the buggy had overturned, or a wheel had busted, or whatever else she could conjure up from her imagination. "Lord, Jesus, take care of my baby," she chanted over and over. The more she prayed, the more irritated Rhoda became.

"Adeline, shush! I gather that 'Lia has had this little unchaperoned outing planned all along. Lord, I love that girl just as if she were my own, but she is just too headstrong for her own good. Believe you me, when she gets home, I am gonna wallop her just as if she were my own."

As Adeline quietly recollected the morning, her momentary sighting of the valise in the buggy, she fell back into the nearest chair, lightheaded. *The satchel. Oh, my Lord, the satchel in the buggy. What has my baby gone and did? It cain't be possible. Mr. Lawson would*

Strangers and Sojourners in a Town Called Penryn:

ADELINE

never. . .daren't. . .oh Lordy, no! He be too old. She be too young. The realization of the situation sapped Adeline's strength, leaving her worn out, sick at heart. With her last bit of energy, she addressed her co-chaperone.

"Mrs. Barnes, can you please send a note to Mr. William? You gotta tell him our baby has done eloped."

Strangers and Sojourners in a Town Called Penryn:

ADELINE

Chapter 21

There is one whose rash words are like sword thrusts, but the tongue of the wise brings healing.
Proverbs 12:18

Six weeks since the elopement. Word sure done spread quick enough. Them gossips having a field day over the waywardness of my Annelia. Townsfolks thinkin' I don't hear their snickering and whispering as I be walking though town. I jes' ignore them all. Those mean old biddies. I bet their own daughters would do the same, iff'n they could 'cept hey all be too ugly for any man. Humph!

The couple had returned after four weeks but did not announce their arrival. Instead, they chose to quietly set up housekeeping on the Lawson family homestead, Clover Valley Ranch. Adeline knew when they were back. One of Mr. Joseph's farm hands had helped deliver the newlywed's furnishings which they had purchased on their honeymoon trip.

My baby be back home. Thank you, Jesus, for bringing Miz 'Lia back safely. Course, I still be mighty upset with

Strangers and Sojourners in a Town Called Penryn:

ADELINE

her and that Mr. Lawson, but I still thankful that she be home. Poor Mr. William, bless his heart. And the widow Barnes. They be upset sump'un fierce.

Adeline, busily scrubbing the children's clothes on the washboard, muttered her thoughts and prayers aloud to no one. *So many changes, Jesus. This new farm of Mr. Joseph and Miz Mary; a new house with so many rooms and floors--still, I thank you Jesus 'cuz one room be all mine.*

I be sometin' sad when I had to move away from Stewart's Flat, but you knowed, Jesus. You knowed that it pained me being so far away from the boarding house, from 'Lia. You knowed Miz 'Lia's plans. And now, Miz 'Lia done live but a stone's throw from this here farm, just over in Clover Valley. I 'member Miz Catheraine done tol' me onct that God has a plan for everyone, even a servant girl like me. I reckon she be right about that. God kept my baby girl close to me, even when she be married. Thank you, Jesus.

Strangers and Sojourners in a Town Called Penryn:

ADELINE

The journey to Clover Valley Ranch took less than 30 minutes. Adeline guided the horse cart around to the back of the house. A large black dog greeted her arrival with a throaty growl-like bark, signaling to the inhabitants of the dwelling that an uninvited guest awaited outside.

The dog's raspy yelp progressed to a continual high-pitched woof-woof-woof as the four-legged guardian encircled the one-horse cart. Adeline remained seated, her shushing to the watchdog going unheeded. Still, no one came outside to check on why the dog was making such a fuss.

Stalemate. Adeline looked down at the dog, looked over at the back door, looked around the unattended property, assessing her next move. As she peered back towards the house, measuring how fast she could reach the door, a movement in the door's window caught her eye.

Well, at least I know'd someone be home. It seems I gots to take the first step.

Cautiously, determinedly, purposefully, Adeline alighted the wooden cart while carrying the wedding present. She skirted the yapping dog, approached the back

Strangers and Sojourners in a Town Called Penryn:

ADELINE

door, raised a trembly fisted hand, and knocked soundly. The now silent guard dog stood by her side, looking at the door in anticipation of its opening.

No response. Resolved to complete her task, Adeline knocked again, and again, and again. No response.

She then boldly pronounced, "I be staying here 'til I gets to talk with you, Miz 'Lia!"

Stalemate over. As 'Lia slowly opened the door, Adeline stepped to the side to allow the door to swing fully open. The dog sped past the new co-owner of the house and promptly plopped down by his master's chair. The two women remained put. 'Lia in the threshold, Adeline on the stoop.

Adeline took stock of 'Lia's appearance from head to toe to assure herself that the now married *child* was not being neglected or mistreated.

"Well, Adeline, I guess father sent you to check up on me. You can tell him that I am fine. He doesn't have to be bothered with me anymore. I warned him I was not going to go back to Sacramento." Although the words were

Strangers and Sojourners in a Town Called Penryn:

ADELINE

scornfully spoken, Adeline could see the pain and sadness in the young bride's eyes.

"Oh, Missy. If only you waited two more weeks. If only. . ."

'Lia, confused by the statement, questioned Adeline. "What do you mean, two more weeks?"

Stammering, Adeline tried to gently reveal the now defunct surprise. "I brought you and Mr. Leonard a wedding present. I started making 'em 'bout two weeks afore you done. . . got married."

'Lia accepted the present; two pillowcases lovingly embroidered with purple lilac flowers. As she fingered the delicate stitching, she shook her head.

"I don't understand, Adeline. Why would you be making pillowcases for me? I had no use for them at the boarding school. And how could you know about my plans to elope?"

"Well, Miz 'Lia, that be part of the surprise." Adeline looked down, avoiding eye contact with 'Lia, speaking almost at a whisper. "The surprise your papa had for you." When she looked back up at 'Lia, Adeline could not stop

Strangers and Sojourners in a Town Called Penryn:

ADELINE

her tear drops from falling. "Oh, Missy. . .Missy. . .Mr. William done built a home for you so you could stay in Stewart's Flat. He was awaitin' for it to be completely done b'fore telling you. It lacked jus' two weeks till being done. Two weeks."

As 'Lia comprehended what Adeline had said, her tears began to fall as well.

"Why didn't he tell me? Why didn't he tell me?"

Adeline embraced the sobbing girl. For once, 'Lia did not reject the comfort given by her former caretaker.

As the sobbing ended, 'Lia parted herself from Adeline. The sorrow and regret of her reckless actions now replaced with an indignant attitude.

"It's all father's fault. He always thinks he knows best. He shouldn't have taken me away after momma died. He was just plain selfish, not wanting to be bothered with me, only visiting me whenever he had to pick up supplies in the city. You think I don't know that he cares more for you than for his own child? He was always more worried about how you were doing than I! How I envied his affection to you." With this last bitter remark, 'Lia took the dain-

Strangers and Sojourners in a Town Called Penryn:

ADELINE

ty pillowcases, threw them in Adeline's face, and tried to slam the door closed.

But Adeline would have none of it. She held the door open, addressing her former charge with a fire in her voice that stopped 'Lia's actions.

"Now you listen here, Missy. Your papa done what he could for you. Twasn't his fault your momma be dead. Twasn't his fault that he couldn't take care of you. Jus' like ain't his fault that I still be a slave even when the Pres'dent say I be free. Your papa cain't change things that happen in life. He jus' cain't. He jus' cain't." Her voice trailed off. The last words spoken in a mournful whisper.

Back to stalemate. No more moves. No more words. Adeline picked up the soiled pillowcases, brushed off the dirt, folded them in quarters, and handed them back to 'Lia. "Happy marriage, Mrs. Lawson. May God bless and keep you and Mr. Leonard." The once beloved nanny then turned her back to her former charge. Tears began to form again in her eyes. Gathering her skirt above her boots, she struggled to get up into the wagon then slowly made her way back to where she belonged—as a slave in the Goldstan household.

**Strangers and Sojourners
in a Town Called Penryn:**

ADELINE

Chapter 22

*Though you have made me see troubles,
many and bitter, you will restore my life again;
from the depths of the earth
you will again bring me up.
Psalm 71:20*

Adeline covered the food basket with a clean flour-sack towel, protecting the still warm contents from flies and other winged creatures that might be attracted to the aroma of the fried chicken, okra, and apple pie. Two pints of fresh buttermilk completed the meal. *Today was su'posed to be a time a cel'bratin'. 'Stead, it feel more like a remem'brin service. Well, I guess Miz 'Lia's running away did stymie Mr. William's hopes of being back together with his daughter and rightin' his wrongs concerning her upbringing.* A loud whinnying and a jerk of the lead rein by the wagon's horse broke through Adeline's thoughts. Her woolgathering over, she slapped the horse's rump with the rein. The steed responded back with a flapping of his lips and a toss of his head. The jang-jang, jang-jang of the wagon wheels cross-

Strangers and Sojourners in a Town Called Penryn:

ADELINE

ing over the newly laid railroad tracks startled the horse. Adeline coaxed the animal along with a "hya-hya."

"C'mon, Jubilee. Mr. William's awaiting!" Today was moving-in day. A day that no longer held significance for the person moving. As Adeline crested the hill leading to William's house, she saw two other wagons descending on the farm, each of them filled with household goods and supplies. Adeline spied the widow Barnes—a passenger of the second wagon which lagged behind the first. Jublilee pricked up his ears at the sight and sound of the other work horses.

"Let's catch 'em, boy!" The horse picked up his pace as Adeline encouraged him onward. Soon, Adeline and Jubilee were traveling side-by-side with Mrs. Barnes and the wagon's driver.

"Afternoon, Miz Rhoda."

Rhoda nodded her head at Adeline in recognition. Bill Isaacs removed his hat, bowed his head slightly, and looked squarely at Adeline. "Hello, Ma'am."

**Strangers and Sojourners
in a Town Called Penryn:**

ADELINE

"Adeline, this is Bill Isaacs." Rhoda introduced the two. "He was hired by William to begin clearing the land and to oversee the planting of the fruit trees."

Adeline couldn't help but notice the comeliness of this stranger; the deep blue eyes, the golden red hair, and the innumerable tawny freckles covering his fair face. Timidly, she replied, "Pleased to meet you, Mr. Isaacs."

Bill put his hat back on his head, adjusting the tilt of it to keep the sun out of his eyes. Adeline now found it hard to see his eyes, hidden by the brim, but she did notice that Bill continued to rubberneck in her direction, his gaze lingering for perhaps too long. An unexpected queasiness came over her—a feeling that she had never experienced before. Embarrassed, Adeline averted her eyes and stared straight ahead.

But her curiosity of the newcomer was stronger than her discomfit. She slowly turned her head to get another glimpse at Bill and found that he was still studying her. This time, Adeline did not look away from this man. *Humph. Who he think he be?*

**Strangers and Sojourners
in a Town Called Penryn:**

ADELINE

The three wagons and passengers neared their destination. William stood on the front porch, waving them on towards the back of the house. He hopped down from the stoop and lead the teams to a shady spot, not far from the informal entrance to the house. Striding over to the wagons, he hollered out, "Welcome, welcome to my farm. Thank you for your help. I most appreciate your kindness."

Bill Isaacs helped the widow Barnes down from the front seat, holding her elbow until she was planted securely on solid ground. Next, he stepped over to help Adeline but she casually waved him off. Ignoring her gesture, Bill placed his hands firmly on her waist as she stepped onto the wheel hub. Adeline paused for a moment, then placed her hand on his shoulder. Bill smiled up at her and gently guided Adeline as she stepped down.

"Thank you, Mr. Isaacs."

"My pleasure, Miss Adeline."

The driver and male passenger of the third wagon laughingly called out, "What about me, *Mr. Isaacs*?"

Bill ignored the scoffing and began unloading the cargo from his wagon. The other men followed suit. Ade-

**Strangers and Sojourners
in a Town Called Penryn:**

ADELINE

line and Rhoda carried the prepared food into the house and began to set the table for the noonday meal. Their task completed, they surveyed the newly built house, both of them knowing the love that had motivated William to build it; both saddened that his attempt to make amends with his daughter had come to naught.

"I like all the furniture you done picked out, Miz Rhoda. Makes a person feel welcome just by coming into the parlor."

The widow sighed. "Thank you, Addie. I chose the pieces with the expectation that 'Lia would be living here with her father. I just pray that William won't sell the place, lock, stock, and barrel, now that his daughter will not be here with him."

"Sell the house? Oh, Miz Rhoda, do you think he might'n? Where would he go? Where would he live?" Adeline tried to control her fear of William leaving Stewart's Flat—of leaving her behind, but her quivering voice betrayed her. She grasped the widow's hands. "We gots to make sure he stays!"

**Strangers and Sojourners
in a Town Called Penryn:**

ADELINE

"I can only try my best, Adeline. You must understand that it is hard for William to stay in a house that was built for one purpose—to reunite a father and daughter."

The sound of the workers entering the dining area brought a halt to any more conversation between the two women. Adeline and Rhoda fetched the ready-made noonday dinner from the kitchen stove and placed the warm serving dishes on the sideboard. The aroma of fried chicken hovered in the air. William invited the men to be seated around the table. He then offered up a short, quick prayer of thanksgiving, said "Amen," and without hesitation proclaimed, "Let's eat!"

The men served themselves, filling their plates with hearty portions. When, at last, they were seated and eating, Rhoda and Adeline served themselves. William pulled out a chair for the widow Barnes. Adeline, carrying her plate, headed for the kitchen.

"Adeline, come back here." William's tone was cordial, not commanding. "Come join us at the table."

The men at the table stopped eating for a moment, looking at William as if he had uttered a profanity.

Strangers and Sojourners in a Town Called Penryn:

ADELINE

William got up, took Adeline's plate from her, placed it on the dining table, offered the startled black woman a chair, helped her be seated, then returned to his chair. As he sat down, he noticed the stillness in the room. Without apology or hesitation he declared, "Adeline is part of my family and will always be welcomed at my house and my table."

Adeline's spirits soared at William's declaration. She placed her hand atop William's, a gesture of familiarity. "Thank you, Mr. William."

William placed his other hand atop Adeline's. "I know this may be hard for you, Addie, but you can just call me William, no need for the Mr. I won't push you to do so, but know here and now that you are not my slave, never have been, and never will be. Catheraine and I began as caretakers for you as we journeyed to California. Somewhere along the way you became a part of our family and you will always remain family." William eyed those seated at the table, conveying the sincerity of his words to his guests. His gaze lingered a bit longer on the widow Barnes as if to gain her approval. She nodded ever-so-slightly in

Strangers and Sojourners in a Town Called Penryn:

ADELINE

acquiescence. William nodded back and heartily ordered, "Now, back to eating!"

Silence, again. Not because of the awkwardness of the situation, but because everyone was too busy enjoying the meal to join in a conversation with their table mates.

Adeline relaxed a bit, emotionally overwhelmed by the unexpected pronouncement. Her position as part of the Barton family was now firmly established and openly declared by the patriarch. She had some misgivings about the reaction of the rest of the town folks as to her new standing in the community. But her main worry concerned Annelia's response. She prayed for the best but prepared for the worst.

Adeline gathered up the dirty dishes and carried them to the kitchen as the well-fed workers retuned to finish up the unloading of the wagons. Mrs. Barnes and William remained seated at the table, discussing the future fate of Stewart's Flat as the townsfolk transitioned from gold mining to rock quarry mining.

"I never thought it would happen, William. The town seemed to be thriving with all the new families that

Strangers and Sojourners in a Town Called Penryn:

ADELINE

moved into the area. To see houses disassembled then re-assembled closer to the quarry and the rail line makes me wonder what will happen to our beloved Stewart's Flat."

William gently placed his hand on Rhoda's. "Change is always hard, my dear. We can either fight against the tide or flow with the current. The town has served its purpose. Many families have profited from the mines, allowing them to buy farmland—to be able to continue to provide for their families long after the gold is gone. Towns are born and towns die, just like friends and loved ones. Those left behind must move forward, must adapt to the metamorphosis, just as the caterpillar emerges from its cocoon as an entirely new creature. All living things, including mankind, must learn to adjust, evolve, transform to the variableness of life. We either change. . .or perish; these are the only choices available to us."

Adeline, overhearing the private conversation, pondered all the things being said by William. She thought of all the changes that she had to accept in her life; being taken from her mother; becoming a servant to Miz Mary; leaving Mississippi for California; grieving the death of Cather-

Strangers and Sojourners in a Town Called Penryn:

ADELINE

ine; the growing disaffection of 'Lia. Twenty-two years of alterations. Twenty-two years of subjugation. Twenty-two years of loss. A loud gasp from the widow Barnes interrupted Adeline's silent reflections.

"William, are you sure?" The tone in the Rhoda's voice conveyed joy but also a bit of hesitation. Adeline peeked around the kitchen door frame just in time to see William pick up Rhoda's left hand and lovingly bestow a kiss upon it.

"Quite sure, my dear. Just tell me when you are ready. I will be waiting."

Adeline stirred in the doorway, catching William's eye. "Come join us, Adeline. There is something I want to share with you."

Adeline sat next to William on the left side, while the widow sat on the right. William took Adeline's hand. "I have asked Mrs. Barnes to marry me. By the twinkle I see in her eyes, I believe she has given me her assent. Since you are family to me, I wanted you to share in this happy matter."

Strangers and Sojourners in a Town Called Penryn:

ADELINE

"Mr. William, er, I mean William, I be pleased to share in your joy."

Rising from the table, Adeline approached the now standing widow and gave her a hug. "Thank you, Miz Rhoda, for bringing happiness back to Mr. William." The widow accepted Adeline's embrace, although Rhoda's returning embrace was a bit stiffer.

"Now," boomed William, "shall we set a date? The sooner the better!"

The widow blushed a crimson red. "Mr. Barton!"

He guffawed. "I am 40-years-old, Mrs. Barnes and not getting any younger!" With this last remark, William stood, drew the 28-year-old widow to him and proceeded to kiss her squarely on the lips.

"William!"

"Just sealing the deal, my dear. . . just sealing the deal. Adeline, you are a witness. There will soon be a wedding," he turned to his speechless fiancé, "and a wedding *night*."

Strangers and Sojourners in a Town Called Penryn:

ADELINE

This last statement proved too much for the modest widow. She bolted for the outdoors. William's laughter followed behind her.

"Oh, Mr. William, why you tease her so?" Adeline tried to refrain from laughing but a giggle managed to escape. They both began to chuckle. He winked at Adeline. "Let's keep this engagement a secret between us three until Mrs. Barnes is ready to make a formal announcement and set a date."

"Yessir, Mr. William." She paused a bit. "Mr. William, it sure be good to see you laugh agin'."

"It has been a long time, Adeline. We have had enough heartaches for this lifetime. May the rest of our days be filled with peace and merriment."

"Yes'm, Mr. William. And may Miss 'Lia be amongst us to share in the joy."

"Amen, Adeline. Amen."

Strangers and Sojourners in a Town Called Penryn:

ADELINE

Chapter 23

*Contend, O Lord, with those who contend with me;
fight against those who fight against me!
Psalm 35:1*

Two weeks later, amid the rumors circulating amongst the townsfolk. Adeline's earlier misgivings about William's proclamation were soon confirmed. News of Adeline's "adoption" into the Barton family spread through the community. Before long, well-meaning citizens, mainly womenfolk, came a-calling on William.

By happenstance, Adeline and Rhoda were visiting at William's house when the procession of concerned residents commenced. William graciously accepted the visitors, parried their questions, addressed their concerns, and gently escorted them out the front door.

From what Adeline could discern, the residents' main concerns centered around whether Adeline had somehow used chicanery on William. After all, she was somewhat appealing "for a colored person". Mr. Barton, a widower for the past eleven years, could have succumbed to

Strangers and Sojourners
in a Town Called Penryn:

ADELINE

his need for womanly comfort. Had Adeline blackmailed William? Her promise of silence in exchange for inclusion into the family—of a certainty of being cared for in the years to come? Unbridled speculation galloped through the women's sewing circles. Why else would a white man claim a full-grown negress as family?

Poor Mr. William. Seem like no matter what good he try and do, it all turns out upside down from what he be intendin'. Why should people be worryin' 'bout me? I ain't gonna bother them. My life be none of their biz'ness—leastways it seemed they twernt caring about it before Mr. William done made me part of the fam'ly.

Another knock at the door. Another well-meaning, God-fearing woman. Adeline crossed the room to open the door but William had had enough. He stopped her before she could reach the doorknob. He bellowed at the closed door, directing his anger to the unwanted caller. "Go away with your concerns! Leave me in peace!" Adeline and Rhoda hurried to stand by the beleaguered man.

The rapping continued. William remained seated at the table.

Strangers and Sojourners in a Town Called Penryn:

ADELINE

The uninvited visitor opened the door slightly. William jumped up, knocking the dining room chair out from underneath him, sending it crashing across the room. As he reached the doorway, he cursed, "Be damned, you meddling fool!" As he spoke the last word, Annelia appeared in the entryway.

"Well, Father. I may be damned and I may be meddling, but I am no fool. Sit down before you have an apoplexy."

Undaunted by her father's outburst, Annelia brushed past the trio of astonished adults, removed her riding gloves and hat, and sat down at the table. "Adeline, could you fetch me a cup of tea? Perhaps one for Father, also. From the looks of him, I think he needs a strong-brewed cup of your darkest leaves. Bring one for Mrs. Barnes, also."

Adeline, startled by the married fifteen-year-old girl's usurping of the situation, simply stated, "Yes'm, Missy." 'Lia turned to reprimand Adeline's impertinence but stopped when she saw the welcoming smile on the servant's face. For the first time in a long while, 'Lia smiled

Strangers and Sojourners in a Town Called Penryn:

ADELINE

back at Adeline and politely replied, "Thank you, Adeline" then turned her attention back to William.

"Now, Father, what is all this nonsense I hear about you and Adeline?"

Father and daughter pow-wowed for over an hour. The intensity of their private conversation permeated the household.

Adeline caught bits and pieces of their exchange as she busied herself by tidying up the kitchen. The widow Barnes had politely recused herself from the father and daughter on the excuse that Adeline needed help in the kitchen. Both women fixated on the conversation while trying to appear indifferent to the tumult.

William's voice increased in volume in proportion to his protest over his daughter's reasonings. "I don't care what all them interfering gossips think! Adeline has been a helper and a faithful friend to me and your departed mother. She has never tried to wangle her way into our lives as so many of those foolish townsfolk suppose."

Strangers and Sojourners in a Town Called Penryn:

ADELINE

"Father, please listen to me. I know firsthand the destructiveness of scandalmongers. These unfounded tittle-tattles must be put to rest."

William fidgeted a bit with the tablecloth. He called towards the kitchen. "Mrs. Barnes, Adeline, please join us."

As the two women nervously entered the room, William turned his attention back to Annelia. "Well, daughter, perhaps a wedding would quash the rumors."

"A wedding? You and Adeline get married? Father, have you lost your senses?!" Annelia glared at the speechless, motionless Adeline. "Look at her! She's an ignorant, uncomely *slave*." These last words lingered, suspended in the air like a noose at the gallows waiting for its victim. Annelia plowed ahead with her uncensored insults, paying no heed to her father's stone-faced countenance.

"Thankfully, a marriage between a white person and a colored one is not legal."

William slammed both of his clenched fists on the dining room table, breaking through his daughter's diatribe. His barely constrained comeback boomed through the small house, rattling the windows like a thunderclap.

Strangers and Sojourners in a Town Called Penryn:

ADELINE

"E—NOUGH, Annelia. Enough! To think that a so-called daughter of mine could be so objectionable! Your own unbecoming conduct of this past year has caused me more shame and distress than any actions ascribed to Adeline. I love you, my daughter, with all my being. But, if I hear you speak one more disparaging word regarding Adeline, in my presence or anyone else's, I will terminate our relationship, permanently and legally. Do you understand?"

The chastened child, silenced by righteous wrath, paled at her father's proclamation. She bowed her head. Her authoritative posture crumbled. Her chin quivered as she hesitantly asked, "You would disown me, in favor of a. . .a. . .of *her*?"

William, so staunch and upright, folded at his daughter's plea. He drew his lost child to his chest. Burying her face in his jacket, she released years-long pent-up tears and sobs. Adeline and Mrs. Barnes witnessed the prodigal daughter's return to her father and the father's whole-hearted forgiveness.

Minutes passed. Annelia looked up at William, smiled at the widow Barnes, nodded at Adeline, and vowed,

Strangers and Sojourners in a Town Called Penryn:

ADELINE

"As long as you live, Father, I will never again speak badly about Adeline. I give you my pledge." The tension in the room evaporated.

William winked at Mrs. Barnes. "Now, about that marriage."

Annelia winced visibly but said not a word. She closed her eyes, preparing herself for the unwelcome announcement.

William continued. "The marriage that is to take place, Annelia, is between myself and Mrs. Barnes."

Relief flooded over Annelia. "Oh, Father, I am so pleased." She hugged William. He hugged back. Neither let go for a full minute. A reconciliation. A truce. A new start.

Adeline turned toward the kitchen. Tears filled her eyes. *It be about time. Thank you, Jesus.*

The next day, Adeline rested on the Goldstan's back porch in her favorite chair, an old wooden rocker. Her hands moving rhythmically, methodically, as she shelled peas for the evening supper. This was one of her preferred

Strangers and Sojourners in a Town Called Penryn:

ADELINE

chores. It gave her a chance to put her feet up plus time to mull over the recent happenings of her life and of those she loved.

Mr. William gonna marry Mrs. Barnes. Hmmmph. I be glad for them both. Miss 'Lia now a married woman. That sure be a s'prise. Thank the Lord that they all be on speakin' terms again. I guess I gots to be thinkin' 'bout Christmas since ev'rybody be comin' here to celebrate. Thank you, Jesus 'cuz I gets to see my 'Lia and her papa together on Christmas day, jus' like my first Christmas time celebratin' with 'em. It be true what the good book say 'bout ,"All things work together for good." Seems all be workin' out here real fine.

She awoke from her daydreaming just in time to see three-year-old Frankie running towards a massive oak tree. "Frankie, you stay away from that there oak! You hear me? I gots no time be fetching you down from that tree onct you gets stuck up there!" Adeline, aware of the boy's youthful daringness and ability to climb any tree, worried for his safety. His climbing adventures always seemed to end up in some sort of mishap. His last escapade resulted in a badly

**Strangers and Sojourners
in a Town Called Penryn:**

ADELINE

sprained ankle which landed him in bed for a week. Adeline had dutifully nursed the little boy back to health, admonishing him to "use the common sense the good Lord done give you" the next time he thought about scaling a tall pine, cottonwood, or oak tree. But the lad continued to shinny up any large tree that he encountered.

Today was no exception. Adeline's warning only fueled Frankie's resolve. He smiled—innocence beaming from his angelic, freckled face—turned away from Adeline, and skedaddled as fast as his three-year-old legs could handle. He reached the towering oak before Adeline could raise herself out of the comfortable rocking chair. He looked back at his caretaker, stuck out his tongue, then jumped up to catch the lowest branch.

"Joseph Landmerac Goldstan, Jr!" Adeline shouted his full name in exasperation. "You be asking for a switchin'!"

"You gotta catch me first, Addie!" He reached for the next branch, then the next, then the next, until Adeline grew fearful at the height of his climb.

Strangers and Sojourners in a Town Called Penryn:

ADELINE

Pleading, cajoling, even bribing the youngster with a molasses cookie all fell unheeded on the ears of the impish boy.

Sighing, her back to the tree, Adeline muttered to herself but intentionally spoke loud enough for Frankie to hear. "I 'spose I gots to go get Mr. Joseph." She slowly ambled towards the field where Joseph was tending to the cattle. Before she had taken five steps, Frankie had joined her, placing his tiny pale hand into Adeline's work-roughened palm. She enclosed her fingers around the boy's trembling hand.

"I came down, Addie. Do you still need to talk to papa?" He hung his head as he spoke softly to her.

They both stopped walking. Adeline bent down to the child to be at eye level.

"Frankie, I jes' be looking out for you, to be sure you cain't get hurt again. It would break my heart if sumptin' really bad happened to my little man." She gathered the child into her arms. "I won't be telling your papa this time. But, you gots to start lis'ning to me. Deal?"

Frankie hugged her neck. "Deal."

Strangers and Sojourners
in a Town Called Penryn:

ADELINE

Adeline held out her hand to the boy. "We gots to shake on it, just like grown-ups do." He grasped the outstretched hand, then energetically shook it. Glancing up at Adeline beseechingly, he added, "Can I still have that cookie?"

Strangers and Sojourners in a Town Called Penryn:

ADELINE

Chapter 24

*Aim for restoration, comfort one another,
agree with one another, live in peace;
and the God of love and peace will be with you.
II Corinthians 13:11*

December, 1867

Friends and family reposed by the fire, allowing their Christmas dinner to settle before partaking of dessert. The younger children, Frankie and Susan, sitting indian-style on the floor, waited anxiously, not for cake or pie but for the gifts to be handed out. Joseph and Mary rested contentedly together on the love seat, holding hands. Newly-wed Annelia joined the children on the floor but at the feet of her husband, Leonard, who rested on a large velvet ottoman. The not-yet-newlyweds, William Barton and Rhoda Barnes, chose the two armchairs that were arranged around a small, round, table by the window. The older children, Thomas and Ella, stood at the perimeter of the group. And behind them all, in the dining room doorway, stood Ade-

Strangers and Sojourners in a Town Called Penryn:

ADELINE

line, observing the tranquil, satiated group. Her gazing lingered upon Annelia, the child-bride. In California, fifteen-year-old brides were not unheard of, but to Adeline, 'Lia was still just a child—too young to start carrying the weight of womanhood, wifehood, and eventually, motherhood. Yet, despite her misgivings, Adeline noted a change in Annelia. A contentedness—a calming of the chaos of the early years. *P'haps Mr. Leonard being so much older than 'Lia has done my little Missy some good and helped settle the pain in her heart.*

    At that moment, Annelia roused from her spot on the floor. She scurried past Adeline and headed through the kitchen and out the back door towards the privy. When she had not come back in some time, Adeline decided to check up on her. She approached the out-house, expecting to see it closed up. Instead, the wooden door swung lazily back and forth, propelled by the gentle winter wind. Annelia was not inside. Adeline scanned the area around the small building. No 'Lia in sight. She listened intently to the stillness of the outdoors and discerned a sound different from the rustling of breeze-tossed leaves and the cheep-cheep of sparrows.

Strangers and Sojourners in a Town Called Penryn:

ADELINE

Adeline walked farther into the grove of oaks, guided by the out-of-place noise. She finally espied Annelia, on her knees, bent over, vomiting the last remains of the contents of her stomach.

Adeline rushed over to the sick girl and cradled Annelia's head while at the same time handing the child bride a hanky. "My poor little Missy, sick on Christmas day. You lean on me, now, chil'. Addie be here to help."

'Lia accepted the hanky and the help. The sickness soon passed and Adeline assisted 'Lia as she staggered to her feet. "Thank you, Adeline." She smoothed her dress, placed a wayward curl back in its place, pinched her cheeks for color, and began walking back to the house. Adeline placed her arm through the girl's arm at the elbow and for once, Annelia did not remove the slave's arm.

"How long you been sick, Miss 'Lia? Not that I mean to intrudes. I jes' wants to make sure you not be catching sump'in fierce." Memories of Catherine's fatal illness surfaced in Adeline's mind.

Annelia looked at Adeline, seeing fear and concern descend on her dark round face. She hesitated in respond-

Strangers and Sojourners
in a Town Called Penryn:

ADELINE

ing to Adeline, but then plunged ahead. "I believe I am alright, Addie. Nothing to worry about. This will pass. . . in seven months or so."

Comprehension. Astonishment. *Almost* speechlessness. "Why, Miss 'Lia, are you. . .are you sure?"

"Yes, Addie. I am sure." Tiredness had crept into her voice. "But, I have not yet spoken to Leonard. I want to spare him from worrying about me for the time being. And I do not want father to worry either. So, I will wait as long as possible to share my condition with anyone else. Do you understand what I am saying?"

Adeline, put back in her place by the young mother-to-be, solemnly nodded. "Yes'm. I won't be telling a soul."

As they reached the back porch, Annelia disentangled her arm from Adeline's. She tossed the soiled hanky back to the servant, sauntered in front of the now immobile Addie, entered the living room, and cheerfully announced, "Mary, I think Adeline is anxious to serve the desserts. Shall we accommodate her?" The group arose en masse and descended upon the heavily laden buffet table, the children leading the way.

Strangers and Sojourners in a Town Called Penryn:

ADELINE

***

Adeline bustled around the kitchen, occupying her time and mind with routine household tasks. Yet, she paused every now and then, placed her hands on her heart, and whispered a prayer heavenward—a supplication for an easy "birthin'" for 'Lia. She worried for the girl. The doctor had confined her to bed early on in the pregnancy. According to him 'Lia was carrying an overly large baby, an omen of a difficult birth. All precautions were taken to ensure the young mother-to-be's safety. 'Lia fought against her forced confinement, but her protests went unheeded. Mary and Rhoda had taken turns supervising the strong-willed 'Lia during this time period, keeping the concerned Adeline posted of the activities.

Mary entertained the invalid by reading to her by reading Lydia Marie Child's "The Mother's Book"; by helping 'Lia sew, knit, and crochet the baby's layette; by keeping the young mother's spirits up with stories of the happenings at Stewart's Flat. Rhoda kept 'Lia occupied by requesting her help in planning the widow's upcoming marriage to William, scheduled for the springtime of 1869,

Strangers and Sojourners in a Town Called Penryn:

ADELINE

eights months away. All these endeavors allowed 'Lia to bear her lying-in.

Adeline envied the time the two women spent with her 'Lia. She would gladly have sat with the temporary shut-in but an invitation to do so never materialized. Time passed, slowly, methodically, through the hot summer months, until the days were completed for Annelia to give birth—August 2, 1868.

Adeline took no notice of the hotness of the day. She continually paced the length of the kitchen, then the length of the back porch, then back into the kitchen, awaiting news of the birth. When she could bear the wait any longer, she called to the children. They gathered round her in the kitchen.

"Chil'ren, I be going to see Miss 'Lia. Mr. Thomas, you be in charge whilst I am away. Miss Susan, Miss Ella, and 'specially you, Mr. Frankie, don't be causing no troubles, you hear?" All replied at once. "Yes'm, Addie."

"Good. Now, I gots to go." Turning her back to the brood, she snatched her walking hat off the peg, tied the strings under her chin, and set out for the Lawson ranch.

**Strangers and Sojourners
in a Town Called Penryn:**

ADELINE

Adeline covered the mile-long walk in record time. As she approached the farmhouse, she noticed Mr. William's wagon parked along the wooden fence, the horse team grazing on the other side. Miss Mary's carriage, along with other unattended wagons, were scattered around the house.

Addie hesitated at the doorway. The boldness of her action to enter the house, uninvited, faded with each moment she remained on the stoop. *Here I be, twenty-three years ole', and still 'fraid of what folks mighten' say 'bout my bein' here, 'bout me knowin' my place.*

Adeline wavered. Her resolve to see Annelia broken down by inward fears. She had a decision to make. Defiant or deferential?

I done watched over Miss 'Lia when she be a baby, when her mama weren't able, when her mama be dyin'. I gots a right to see her. The chile' might'n be disagreeable with me now-a-days, but I still gots to make sure she be takin' care of. 'Sides, the most anybody can say is tell me to leave.

**Strangers and Sojourners
in a Town Called Penryn:**

ADELINE

Adeline purposefully removed her hat, willfully opened the door, and boldly walked into the house.

None took notice of her entrance. She found Mr. William and the nervous papa-to-be listening intently to the attending doctor. Adeline moved closer to the group in hopes of hearing their discussion, praying that all was will with the young mother. The attending physician reassured the worried men.

"No need to worry, William. Your daughter is well equipped for bearing children. And Leonard, your wife sends her love and is quite eager to be able to present a son to you soon."

Both men collapsed back into their chairs, their relief of this news apparent on their relaxed postures and faces. As the doctor returned to the birthing bedroom, Adeline cleared her throat, drawing the men's attention away from the physician and towards her.

"'Scuse me, Mr. William, but I had to know how Missy 'Lia be doin'."

William raised up from his now comfortable position and strode over to her. Encircling his arm round her

Strangers and Sojourners in a Town Called Penryn:

ADELINE

shoulders, he gave her a comforting hug. "'Lia is doing fine, Addie. The doctor says that she is strong, in good health, and quite capable of coming through the birthing process without any complications."

"Yes'm, Mr. William." She turned towards Leonard. "Mr. Leonard, is there sumpin' I could gets you while you be waiting?"

Leonard waved impatiently at Adeline, dismissing her without saying a word.

William took the silenced servant by the elbow and led her back to the kitchen area. "Adeline, you mustn't be bothered by Leonard's actions right now. He is distressed by his wife's discomfort and pain, fearful that she may be in danger, despite the doctor's opinion to the contrary."

"Yes'm, Mr. William. But, I be worried, too. Ain't no matter that I jes' be an outsider to everyone here. I still love and worry for my baby girl."

At that moment, Mary entered the kitchen, took the hot tea-kettle off of the stove, and hurriedly carried it back to 'Lia's bedroom—all without noticing or acknowledging William or Adeline.

Strangers and Sojourners in a Town Called Penryn:

ADELINE

"I believe the time is almost here, Adeline. Come, you can join me in the waiting room." Walking back to the parlor, he chuckled a bit. "Just think, I am about to be a grandpa. Me, at the ripe-old-age of 41. And next year, a bride-groom. Who knows, there might be another birth in store for me in the near future." This time he laughed out loud. Adeline grinned at Mr. William's ruminations. *I guess it be possible—the widow Barnes being just 30-year-old, well, 31 by the time of the weddin'.*

A baby's cry interrupted her thoughts. Leonard rose from his chair and started towards the bedroom. The babe cried again, a loud and determined-to-be-heard cry. Soon, the cries resounded through the house, echoing off wooden walls, sounding more like a passal of infants instead one small newborn. Leonard knocked on the bedroom door, awaiting admittance. "Hold on out there! I will let you know when you can come in!" The doctor shouted out his orders to the new father. "I still got work to do here!"

Adeline could hear her mistress's and the widow Barnes' excited utterances over the new-born baby. She and

**Strangers and Sojourners
in a Town Called Penryn:**

ADELINE

William drew closer to the door to make out what was being said.

"Look at those feet! He is going to grow up big and tall like his daddy!"

"Such a head of hair. What a sight!"

"And look at this one's feet—no where near the size of his brother's."

All three outsiders glanced at one another. Now, quizzical looks replaced the once concerned expressions that had graced their faces.

Without hesitation, all three knocked on the door. One of the attending women cried out, "For mercy's sake, William and Leonard! Give us a minute, please!"

Eventually, Mary and Rhoda (the widow Barnes) emerged from the room, each carrying a swaddled bundle.

The trio of demanding bystanders now stood in complete silence.

Mary announced, "Leonard, may I present to you your son, Edward Leonard Lawson."

Strangers and Sojourners in a Town Called Penryn:

ADELINE

Rhoda added, "And, may I present to you your son, Garrett Edwin Lawson. Twins, born this day, August 2, 1868."

A fervid voice called from the bedroom. "Leonard. Leonard? Are you all right?"

William stepped up to Leonard, placed a hand on the flabbergasted father's back, and gently pushed him towards the bedroom. "Go see your wife, Leonard. And give her a kiss from me."

Miss Mary's babies all growin' up. Missy 'Lia's baby boys just beginning this life. Mr. William and Miz Rhoda gonna be starting all over again. And me? Adeline sighed, exhaling slowly. *Me? No marriage for me. No babies for me. No home of my own for me.*

An unquenchable yearning for more out of life had enveloped Adeline ever since the birth of the twins. She dreaded change, any kind of change that distanced herself from William and 'Lia. Therefore, she dreaded the upcoming wedding of Mr. William to the widow Barnes. Adeline loved William as a daughter loves a father, wanting only

Strangers and Sojourners in a Town Called Penryn:

ADELINE

the best for him. But, once he was married, she knew her position in his life would change. His new wife's demands would curtail William's impromptu visits with Adeline. She was sure of that. *No woman wants her man to be spendin' time with another female, no matter what color she be.* Another sigh. *I be twenty-three-years-old, and my life will be the very same way when I be eighty, if'n I should live that long. This whole worl' be changin' around me, yet here I sits, the same yesterday as today as tomorrow as forever.*

Even the town of Stewart's Flat kept moving, changing, altering. The marriage of William and Rhoda took place, as planned, on March 21, 1869, under an oak bower in the courtyard in the center of the once flourishing town. The townspeople gathered round the square, delighting in the ceremony, looking forward to the reception. Annelia stood as a witness for her father and the widow Barnes. The Lawson twins, now eight-months-old, were held firmly in tow by their exasperated father, Leonard. Throughout the reception, whenever Adeline tried to help

Strangers and Sojourners in a Town Called Penryn:

ADELINE

with the toddlers, Annelia would shake her head at the willing servant, disregarding Adeline's assistance. So, Adeline wandered to the outskirts of the plaza, noting the alterations that had taken place. She walked up and down the streets, counting fifteen broken-down foundations, tombstones of former buildings. *The postal office, gone. People's homes, gone.* Adeline wandered further out. *'Spose it soon be just a town graveyard, full of memories but no one be living here no more.* Adeline bowed her head, remembering how her new life in California began in this once booming town. So many changes. So many hopes. So many disappointments. So many heartaches.

She continued her pilgrimage. The well-worn pathway directed her past the town's borders, leading her to the outskirts of town, gently guiding her to the graveyard, to Catheraine's final resting place. Adeline knelt by the overgrown gravesite, pulling at the invasive weeds.

Miz Cathy, I be sorry 'bout it being so long since I come to visit. So much has done passed. Little 'Lia now married and a mama. Mr. William marryin' agin. The townsfolks movin' up the hill. I reckon the whole town be

Strangers and Sojourners in a Town Called Penryn:

ADELINE

movin' up there soon. It be perplexin' that things can change for towns and buildings as well as people. Everything and everyone, changin'—'cept for me. . .and 'cept for you."

Adeline witnessed firsthand the fulfillment of her premonitions. Griffith's Granite Quarry grew in size and recognition, requiring more and more laborers to process the growing demands for high quality rock, creating new job opportunities for the out-of-work gold-miners. To be closer to their place of employment, the workers disassembled their wooden homes in Stewart's Flat, reassembling them closer to the quarry.

With the completion of the railroad depot on the Central Pacific Railroad Line, the relocation of Stewart's Flat Mercantile Emporium soon followed. On one Saturday afternoon, the inhabitants of the migrating town undid the nearly vacant Stewart's Flat Hotel, rebuilding it within a block of the busy train station. Ultimately, with the relocation of the saloon, the death knell sounded loud and clear for the once industrious Stewart's Flat—leaving behind the

Strangers and Sojourners in a Town Called Penryn:

ADELINE

silent sentinels of the graveyard to stand watch on the forsaken town.

**Strangers and Sojourners
in a Town Called Penryn:**

ADELINE

Chapter 25

*Father of the fatherless and protector of widows
is God in his holy habitation.
God settles the solitary in a home;
Psalm 68:5-6*

Three years come and gone since the birth of them twins and now Miss Annelia be preparing herself for another birthing. I be happy for her, but, Lord forgive me, I be a mite jealous. Adeline lay in bed, thinking of the day to come, of the chores to be completed, of the children to be fed, of the routineness to be endured. This morning, the morning of September 9, 1872, appeared to be no different than the last, and the last before that, and the last before that.

She stood patiently near the dining table, ready to serve breakfast. Most of the family, already seated at the table, waited not-so-patiently for their Papa to join them. Eight-year-old Frankie fidgeted. Next to him sat thirteen-year-old Susan, muttering to herself, engrossed in reading a newly purchased novel. Across the table from Susan, six-

Strangers and Sojourners in a Town Called Penryn:

ADELINE

teen-year-old Ella fussed with her hair. Nineteen-year-old Thomas nervously drummed his fingers on the tabletop. And Mary, her thoughts irritated by her children's seemingly small commotions, startled the dining room occupants with an abrupt, "SHHUUSH!"

"Thomas, go get your father. It seems he has forgotten about joining us for breakfast today." Under her breath, Mary uttered her displeasure at her husband's memory lapse. "The first day of school—how could he forget?"

Thomas stood, ready to go fetch his father, his action interrupted by a stablehand who had entered the dining room and began knocking not-too-softly on the doorjamb. Having gotten Mary's attention, he solemnly approached her, holding his work cap in his hands, twisting it back and forth. All eyes fixated on the man's actions and demeanor. An uneasy quietness filled the room.

Adeline moved towards the uninvited workman. Mary held up her hand to stop her.

"It's alright, Adeline. I will handle this." She placed her napkin on her plate and stood up at the same time. She indicated for the laborer to follow her into the back porch.

Strangers and Sojourners
in a Town Called Penryn:

ADELINE

He silently followed with head bowed. A few moments passed.

"Miss Mary! Miss Mary!" The workman's beseeching holler reached Adeline's ear. She rushed to the back of the house. Mary lay crumpled on the porch, her face the color of whitewash paint. The workman started to pick up the unconscious woman but Adeline stopped him. Instead, she grabbed a wet washcloth from a nearby water basin and applied the cold compress to Mary's forehead.

By now, all the children had gathered round their mother, fear visibly showing on their faces.

"What you say to Miss Mary?" Adeline barked out the question to the worker while gently cradling her mistress's head. The man began to cry.

The normally soft-hearted Adeline slapped the workman's face, breaking the man's stupor. She yelled, "What is wrong? Tell me! What happened?"

A sob broke from the man. "It is Mr. Joseph, Adeline. We . . .we. . . we went lookin' for 'im when he didn' come back from checkin' on the cattle. We found 'im, just. . .just laying on the ground, 'is eyes wide open towards the

**Strangers and Sojourners
in a Town Called Penryn:**

ADELINE

sky. . .he. . .there was no life in 'im. . . I tried to wake 'im, but. . .but. . ." His tears now flowed freely. The children, in a state of shock from the tragic announcement, looked at one another, heads shaking in disbelief. Adeline, still supporting Mary, began to moan. In unison, the children knelt down beside her, weeping along with Adeline.

Adeline forced herself to gain composure as her common sense returned. "Thomas. *Thomas*!" She called the oldest sibling out of his grief. "Thomas. Go on and fetch Mr. William. He be knowing what to do." She turned to the stunned worker. "Where is Mr. Joseph?"

He collected himself, wiped his eyes, and answered quietly. "I got two of the hands to take a wagon down to the far pasture. They should be here, soon—with Mr. Joseph, ma'am."

Mary started to rouse from her faint. Seeing her children around her, the tears in their eyes, she uttered, "Oh, my poor Joseph. My Joseph."

Adeline stepped into action. "Children, help me get your mother to bed." The older girls took Mary by the arms. After she was able to get on her feet, Frankie put his

Strangers and Sojourners in a Town Called Penryn:

ADELINE

arm around his momma's waist. Together, Adeline and the children helped guide the shaking woman into her bedroom.

The group gently placed Mary onto her bed. The oldest daughter, Ella, bent down and unlaced her mother's shoes. As she gently removed the leather slippers, Ella's free-flowing tears fell onto the red floor cloth, leaving salty spots as they dried.

Once Mary was settled, Ella shepherded Susan and Frankie into the parlor. Together they waited for Thomas to return with Mr. William and give them instructions on what to do next. Adeline hurried out to the yard, awaiting William's coming. She spotted him in the distance riding alongside the lumbering wagon that carried Joseph's body. Thomas flanked the other side. The driver and passenger of the wagon, along with William and Thomas, removed their hats and held them to their chests as they approached the farm house. Adeline walked out to meet the wagon, reverently joining in the procession of bringing Mr. Joseph home.

* * *

Strangers and Sojourners
in a Town Called Penryn:

ADELINE

Adeline handed Mary the requested pair of scissors. She watched as her mistress cut out the article from the newspaper. When she had finished, she passed the cutout to Adeline.

"Please put that in my remembrance book, Adeline. I will fasten it later. Also, I won't be down for dinner tonight. Tell the children that I am weary and need to retire early."

"Yes'm. Would you like dinner in your room?"

"No, thank you. I still can't seem to get my appetite back. However, I will take a cup of hot tea."

"Yes'm. The tea be ready in 'bout ten minutes." Adeline quietly shut the door as she exited. She placed the paper cutting between two pages of Mary's book, smoothing out a few of the book's wrinkled edges. *It sure was nice to say such things 'bout Mr. Joseph in the paper. Thomas be so proud of reading 'bout his papa last night.*

As Adeline closed the memory book, she pictured last night. The family and friends of Joseph had gathered in the parlor to have a time of honoring the man who had died much too young. That was when Thomas had read the

Strangers and Sojourners
in a Town Called Penryn:

ADELINE

memoriam aloud and Adeline finally found out what had been written about the 45-year-old master of the house.

Placer Herald
September 28, 1872

Memoriam—Joseph Landmerac Goldstan

At a stated meeting of Eureka Lodge No. 16. F. & A.M., held Sept. 16,1872, the following preamble and resolutions were adopted:

<u>Whereas,</u> It has pleased the Supreme Grand Architect of the Universe to remove from our midst by death, our es teemed brother Joseph Landmerac Goldstan, and

<u>Whereas,</u> Our duty as Masons, as well as feelings of friendship and sympathy, prompt us to give expression to our grief for our loss, and to console with his family and friends, therefore be it

<u>Resolved,</u> That, by the death of Bro. Goldstan this lodge has lost an upright and worthy Brother, the community an esteemed and valued

**Strangers and Sojourners
in a Town Called Penryn:**

ADELINE

citizen, and his family a kind, a provident husband and father,

<u>Resolved,</u> That the sincere, heartfelt sympathy of the lodge is tendered to his family in this the time of their afflic tion,

<u>Resolved,</u> That these resolutions be published in the local papers and <u>Masonic Manor</u>, and a copy furnished the family of the deceased; and that the lodge room be draped in mourning for thirty days.

Back to the present. Adeline offered up a prayer for the family. *Jesus, give Miss Mary strength. Give the chil'ren peace. Ease their inward pain. And Jesus, help me to be a comfort to ev'ryone. Amen.*

"Chores still gots to be done." Adeline spoke aloud—goading herself into action. She took up a broom and attacked the dirt that had settled into the corners of the kitchen. But her mind wandered while her hands worked. *Sixteen years done come and gone since Miss Catheraine's death, but I still feels it—and me being 26-year-old and*

**Strangers and Sojourners
in a Town Called Penryn:**

ADELINE

growed. I guess I always be feeling her passin'. It'll be the same for Miss Mary. And for the chil'ren. Time passin' will help, but the rememberin' will always be.

Life at the Goldstan ranch returned to normal; as well as normal could be without the much loved head of household. Thomas postponed, indefinitely, his attending the University of California in order to oversee his father's estate. The younger children resumed school attendance a month after the funeral. Visitors called at the house to offer Mary advice on how to endure the first few months of being alone. When not bothered by visitors, Mary spent all her time in her room. She made an appearance at breakfast and suppertime, for benefit of the children, but rarely involved herself in any other activities. Adeline assumed Mary's duties—making sure that all the household needs were met along with all the occupants' needs. And life continued on.

During those long weeks of mourning, Adeline took notice that Mary's heart and attitude towards her had softened. Her mistress now relied on the ever present servant to

Strangers and Sojourners in a Town Called Penryn:

ADELINE

see her through each day. She consulted Adeline about seemingly trivial matters, as if she could not trust herself to make the correct decisions. When not enclosed in her bedroom, she would join Adeline in the kitchen: sometimes just having a cup of tea while Adeline cooked and other times actually helping with the cooking.

Unused to being so needed by Mary, Adeline relished this newly formed intimacy between owner and housekeeper. A fragile bond had formed out of the fetters of grief.

***

The holiday season was soon upon the family, though none felt like celebrating. The veil of mourning that had been drawn on the household was not so easily lifted. For young Frankie's sake, the family observed the Christmas season. Yule tide decorations, put in place by Adeline, helped to lift a bit of the sadness that had settled in the house.

Christmas day. After an early morning breakfast, the family gathered quietly in the parlor. At Mary's request, Adeline joined them. As each child opened their presents,

Strangers and Sojourners
in a Town Called Penryn:

ADELINE

they remarked on the thought that had gone into their parents' choice of gifts.

Thomas opened his gift and glanced down at the book. He lifted his head and looked out the window. To stop tears from falling, he began biting his lower lip. His mother quite came to her oldest child's side, tenderly embracing the emotional young man. "Your father ordered this for you on his last trip to Sacramento. He wanted to present it to you on the day you left for college." Thomas lovingly ran his hand over the much sought-after mineralogy textbook.

"Your father desired for you to follow your dream, just as he had done when he came to California. I agree with your father. You cannot put your life and aspirations on hold for my benefit. I expect for you to begin your studies in the fall and you will comply." With Mary's gentle admonishment to her eldest son over, she turned to her other children.

"Children, I know that we are all grieving our loss. Some days it seems like it never happened—that Papa will walk through the door, ready to join us for dinner." Mary

Strangers and Sojourners in a Town Called Penryn:

ADELINE

paused, then proceeded. "The direction of this family has been irrevocably altered. I am now responsible for our future. I wish to share with you the path that I have chosen for us—my gift to you. While this may be hard to hear, I feel that the sooner you were aware of the plans, the more time it will allow you to prepare for the changes to come."

She nodded towards Thomas. "Thomas will remain with us through the summer," Mary checked her voice then rushed the second part of this announcement, " . . .in order to help with the selling of the farm."

The children, stunned by this announcement, gasped, "What?" Mary continued, ignoring her younger children's outbursts. "In the fall, he will attend the university as planned."

Ella spoke up for the rest of the children. "But, Mother, if we sell the farm, how will we support ourselves and where shall we live?"

Mary smiled at her pragmatic and logical daughter. "My dear sensible Ella. So much like your father." Mary sat down on the nearest chair. "There are plenty of funds to sustain us for a long while. When your father sold the gold

Strangers and Sojourners in a Town Called Penryn:

ADELINE

mine, he invested half of the profits into our farm. The other half has been held for us at a bank in Sacramento."

Perplexed by this answer, Ella asked, "Then why do we need to sell?"

Thomas, deflecting the inquiry away from his mother, carefully answered. "I think I know why. The cost and energy of operating a farm are far more than Mother has the strength to endure. She needs a place to recuperate as do all of you." Mary's weary countenance lifted at her son's insightful words and understanding.

"Where are we moving to, Mother?" This time, Susan softly voiced the question.

Mary knelt down among her children, gathering them into her arms. "My sister-in-law has offered us a place to stay for as long as we need. Although it is quite far from here, I have heard that it is just the spot we need to allow time to heal our hurts. It is near the ocean in a place called Pacific Grove." As outwardly distressed as the children were to Mary's news, Adeline was inwardly disquieted.

Moving? Again? I cain't. Not this time. I gots to find a way to stay. A memory crept into her mind; something

Strangers and Sojourners in a Town Called Penryn:

ADELINE

someone had whispered to her many years ago. *"California be a free state, honey. Ain't ever forgit. If you still be in California when you be growed, you ain't haf to be no one's slave!"* Adeline retreated swiftly towards the back door determined to find a way to remain behind. Her movement caught Mary's eye. "Adeline, please wait." Adeline stopped and faced her mistress, steeling herself against the words to come, wondering how she could graciously defy her owner.

"Yes'm, Miss Mary."

Mary rose up from the floor and approached Adeline. Taking both of Adeline's hands in hers, she brought Adeline into the center of the parlor.

"Adeline, you have been an obedient servant to me for over 20 years. But over these past few months, I have come to see you as a loving caretaker for me and my children."

Astonished as such recognition from Mary, Adeline remained silent.

"I know that you have a strong bond with William Barton. I know that both he and Catheraine loved you as a daughter. I never could comprehend their affection for a,

Strangers and Sojourners in a Town Called Penryn:

ADELINE

um, for someone of your kind until Joseph's passing. It was only then, when I experienced your kindness and compassion, when I didn't deserve such familial treatment, that I came to understand their fondness for you. William and Catheraine saw your heart and not your color. Please forgive me for not recognizing the truth sooner."

Adeline, formerly astonished, now stood open-mouthed at Mary's confession.

Mary forged ahead. "I invite you to join me and my family in Pacific Grove. However, the choice is yours to make. You are no longer my property but, hopefully, a friend. I only ask that you stay with us until we are ready to move."

Adeline started to answer but before she could say two words, she was interrupted by a loud knock at the front door. The visitor burst into the home before being invited in.

"Mary! Come quick! Annelia's gone into labor and she wants you by her side!" Leonard Lawson managed to exclaim his request then rushed back out the opened door, jumped on his horse, and galloped off towards his ranch.

Strangers and Sojourners in a Town Called Penryn:

ADELINE

Thomas hurried to the stables to hitch-up a wagon for his mother.

Mary grasped Adeline's arm and pulled her out the door. "Come, Addie, let's go help Catheraine's daughter."

Six days. Six days of travail. Adeline and Mary lingered at 'Lia's bedside. The doctor slept in the chair in the corner of the room. Leonard, emotionally exhausted from the near weeklong ordeal, sat on a stool at the foot of the bed, endeavoring to remain awake. At the moment, Annelia rested fitfully, the labor pangs having subsided for a time. Leonard, concerned at the length of the birthing process, abruptly roused the doctor from his slumber.

"Doctor, she can't go on much longer. Something must be done." The doctor got to his feet.

"You are right, Mr. Lawson. This has been a very painful delivery for your wife, but I am certain that the time is near for this baby to be born." As the doctor examined 'Lia, those in the room turned their heads away in decorum.

Placing a stethoscope on the largest part of Annelia's stomach, the physician began muttering. "Mmm.

Strangers and Sojourners in a Town Called Penryn:

ADELINE

Yes. . . .". Turning to the embarrassed audience, he announced, "Leonard, it appears that your wife has another surprise in store for you. Twins, *again!*"

Annelia, roused from her twilight sleep by a severe contraction, wearily declared, "I think the time has finally come, Doctor."

"Thank you, Jesus." Adeline voiced what the others were thinking. The weary husband left the room and waited in the parlor for the ordeal to be completed.

William Barton Lawson entered the world on December 31, 1872. His brother, Charles Mortimer Lawson, not wanting to share the same birthdate, waited twenty minutes before making his appearance on January 1, 1873.

Adeline, exuberant at being present at the birthing, counted her blessings that this new year had brought and still had to bring.

Adeline kept track of the number of months until the move—the long, prayed-for move into the Barton home. *January, gone. Feb'rary, gone. March, gone. April.* She celebrated her 28th birthday in April, alone, but not

Strangers and Sojourners in a Town Called Penryn:

ADELINE

unhappy. It seemed that nothing would ever dampen her spirits again since her hopes and dreams were about to realized. *May, gone. June.*

Ever since Miss Mary's blessing of freedom, the now freed black woman's spirits soared. By June of 1873, it seemed that Adeline could not stop smiling. Preparing heaps of cakes and pies and cookies and apple brown bettys for the town's first community party kept her occupied until moving day. As she frosted her favorite baked good, apple cake, her thoughts wondered to the upcoming event. *Penryn. Such an odd name. Not "Griffith's Station" as some done supposed it would be. Hmmm.*

It sounds as as *if the entire town's inhabitants are gonna be present at the ceremony. Even leg'slaters of the State of California be journeying from Sacramento to preside over the ceremony.* Reigning in her thoughts, Adeline tallyed up the copious desserts for the celebration, but her mind wandered once again, this time centering on the days remaining with Miss Mary. *June, almost gone. Only two more months. Only two more months to a new life at Mr. William's and Miss Rhoda's house, praise Jesus!*

Strangers and Sojourners in a Town Called Penryn:

ADELINE

One more month...

One more week...

One more day...

Strangers and Sojourners in a Town Called Penryn:

ADELINE

Chapter 26

*For there is a time and a way for everything,
although man's trouble lies heavy on him.
For he does not know what is to be,
for who can tell him how it will be?
Ecclesiastes 8:6*

**Barton Ranch
Springtime, 1875**

Carrying a straw basket, Adeline strolled leisurely through the orchard, her eyes beholding the varied shades of the plum and peach blossoms; eighty acres of flowering fruit trees that displayed the colors of a painter's palette. *Two years since I be livin' here and I still be in awe.* She never tired of the beauty of this land, the sweet scent of the blooms that burst forth each spring, the summertime harvesting of the bounty of the trees, the endless canning of the fruit, the enjoyment of tasting the preserved food during the cold and rainy winter season. She caroled while ambling midst the rows.

Strangers and Sojourners in a Town Called Penryn:

ADELINE

"Praise God, from Whom all blessings flow; Praise Him, all creatures here below; Praise Him above, ye heavenly host; Praise Father, Son, and Holy Ghost."

A hearty "Amen" resounded from a worker hidden by the trees. Adeline, alerted to the man's presence, changed directions towards the voice.

"There you be, Mr. Isaacs. I done bring your dinner."

Bill Isaacs drew a handkerchief from his shirt pocket, wiped his forehead free from salty drops of sweat then returned the cloth back to its rightful resting place. "Thank you, Addie." He took the basket from Adeline, inadvertently brushing the back of her hand with the calloused palm of his hand during the process.

"You ought to be wearing gloves, Mr. Isaacs."

"Me? Wear gloves? Hah. How could I feel the the tree branch with my hands covered in leather?"

"Why you want to feel a branch?"

"Oh, Addie, there's so much you need to learn and experience. The newly formed boughs and leaves are so

Strangers and Sojourners in a Town Called Penryn:

ADELINE

soft and supple, they feel like the skin of a newborn baby, just waiting to be caressed."

Adeline, confused by his poetic explanation murmured, "You be a strange one, Bill. . .I mean Mr. Isaacs."

"Why, Adeline, you actually called me by my first name. I have been wanting you to do so for the longest time." He proceeded with care. "If you don't mind my asking, how old are you, Addie?"

She thought on his question for a bit, debating whether to allow her personal life to be discussed with this man. Puzzled at his inquisitiveness and out of curiosity as to where the conversation was headed, she answered. "I be thirty, Mr. Isaacs."

Bill 'tsk tsked'. "Thirty. No longer a maiden, but too young to be a spinster."

For some reason, his remark rankled Adeline. "I ain't be no spinster. I jes' happen to not have a husband, *yet*." Her emphasis on 'yet' betrayed her here-to-fore unspoken longing and desire.

Bill grinned at her feistiness. He moved closer to her. "I am sorry, Addie. I meant no offense. I merely want

Strangers and Sojourners in a Town Called Penryn:

ADELINE

to get to know you, as a friend. Can we be friends, Adeline? Will you call me Bill instead of the oh-so-formal Mr. Isaacs?"

Adeline, confused by the inappropriateness of his request, remained silent.

"Listen, Addie, at least when we are alone, will you call me Bill?"

Friends? He wants us to be friends, apart from working for Mr. William?

"I will be thinking on it—Bill." Her reddened face, imperceptible to Bill by her dark skin, burned with embarrassment. She turned and scurried back to the house, disconcerted by this newly formed relationship.

***

"Adeline, are you ready?" the question more of a command, than an inquiry.

"Yes'm, Miz Rhoda. I jes' needs to get a cover for the food."

"Well, quit dawdling. The horses are hitched and William is awaiting for us!"

Strangers and Sojourners in a Town Called Penryn:

ADELINE

"Yes,m! I be right there!" Adeline struggled to lift the fruit crate laden with a prepared dinner as William appeared in the doorway, ready to holler at the two behind-time women. Seeing the cause of the delay, he stepped over and lifted the weighty crate from Adeline arms.

"You should have told me that you needed some help, Addie."

"Yes,m' Mr. William. I jes' thought I could handle it." Rhoda emerged from her bedroom, scuttling through the parlor, fastening the backs to her earrings at the same time.

William bellowed, "Woman, hurry it on up."

Rhoda answered back, mockingly, "Yes, sir, Mr. Barton" then broke into laughter.

"I swear, William, you would think that this was the first time for 'Lia to give birth instead of her third." Rhoda walked past her husband, out the door, and climbed up onto the wagon. "Are you coming, dear?"

"Hmmph. Women." William carried the box to the wagon and placed it on the floorboard. Adeline followed

Strangers and Sojourners in a Town Called Penryn:

ADELINE

closely behind and settled herself in the bed of wagon, next to the crate.

As William clambered onto the front seat, he gave the reins a quick flick to the horse teams' rumps. Rhoda laughed again. "Really, William. No need to take it out on the horses."

"Woman, be silent!" Seeing that the reprimand had no effect on his wife, he chuckled. "I guess I know when I am licked."

"At last, a girl for Missy 'Lia." Adeline beamed at the infant being held by her grandpapa William.

"And not twins!" The proud grandpa cuddled the newborn. "Rachael Hester Lawson, welcome to your family, this nineteenth day of May, in the year of our Lord, 1875. Amen."

Six-year-old twins Edward and Garrett, along with two-and-a-half-year-old twins William and Charles, crowded around their "gm'pa", and gazed at the tiny, sleeping, new-born baby girl. Every now-and-then, one of them

Strangers and Sojourners in a Town Called Penryn:

ADELINE

would lightly touch the infant's wooly-haired head, petting it like they would a fuzzy kitten.

"She be beautiful, Mr. William. Jes' like her mama."

William offered up the newborn to her. "Come, Adeline. Hold her for a spell." She gently cradled baby Rachael in her arms, humming a lullaby to herself—the same lullaby that she had sang to Annelia so many years ago. The same lullaby that Catheraine had taught Adeline twenty-three years ago in Indiana. *Dear Jesus, how I wisht for me my own baby to hold. Iff'n it be your plans for me to marry and have a baby, can it be soon? Iff'n it ain't, please take this longin' away from me 'cuz sometimes it be more than I can bear. I ain't be complainin', Lord. I give thanks for Mr. William and Miz Rhoda bein' my family and takin' me in. But a baby. . .my own flesh. . .well, Jesus, you be knowin' how I feel.* Adeline smiled down at the sleeping child. *Amen.*

**Strangers and Sojourners
in a Town Called Penryn:**

ADELINE

Chapter 27

*I am my beloved's, and his desire is for me.
Song of Solomon 7:10*

'Bout time Mr. William and Miz Rhoda have a honeymoon. Only took 'em seven years. Guess they had to waits until Miz 'Lia not be with child afore they could go.

Adeline hummed loudly as she fried up an egg and some bacon for herself. This was the first time that she was truly in charge of her own person—able to do what she wanted when she wanted. No worrying about meals for others. No worrying about Rhoda finding new chores for her to do. No worrying about doing the laundry on a specific day and in a specific way.

I think that after breakfast, I jes' gonna take me a walk. I been wantin' to see the new plum trees that Mr. William done planted. Maybe I'll take my basket. There just might be some berries ready for the picking'. Hmm. A berry cobbler sure would be nice for after supper.

Strangers and Sojourners in a Town Called Penryn:

ADELINE

She adjusted the well-worn sun hat on her head, tied the hat's leather cords securely under her chin, picked up the berry-stained straw basket, and ambled out the back door. No need to hurry. She had all day to wander through Mr. William's eighty acres, searching out the stickery vines that produced the plump, purple-black fruit.

She moseyed through the growing orchard planted with acres of plum trees, peach trees, apple trees, cherry trees, and orange trees. She took note of the workers who had nearly completed clearing another plot of ground for the soon-to-be-planted mandarin trees. They did not stop working to acknowledge her, but their foreman did.

Bill Isaacs raised his hat and winked. "Miss Adeline. A pleasure to see you." He sauntered towards her.

Adeline glanced up at Bill then slowed her walk. *Should I talk with him? Seein' I be alone and there be workers around?* She knew what the protocol should be in this situation. While Bill and she had conversed, informally, many times since that day when they had become "friends", meeting and conversing so casually in front of the other workers might give the wrong impression.

Strangers and Sojourners in a Town Called Penryn:

ADELINE

"Good morning, Mr. Isaacs. That new field sure be cleared right soon. Cain't wait for them mandarins to start growing. Mr. William say they be better than oranges." She centered the conversation on everyday farm things. Nothing personal. Nothing casual.

Bill Isaacs ignored the rules of propriety. He continued towards her.

"Miss Adeline, how many times have I told you to call me Bill? After all, we are old friends by now. There is no need of formalities between us. Although Mr. Barton did tell me to watch after you while he and the missus are away, I hate to have you think of me solely as a caretaker. I prefer to be thought of as an old family acquaintance." Bill had caught up to Adeline as he made made this last statement. He stood squarely in front of Adeline, carefully watching her face. Adeline kept her head level but gazed past Bill, avoiding eye contact with the becoming gentleman.

He gently took Adeline's hand. "Adeline, I told you, I am your friend. Have faith in me."

Strangers and Sojourners in a Town Called Penryn:

ADELINE

Adeline whispered, "I know, Mr. Isaacs, that we now be 'quantances, but I cain't be calling you Bill in front of the others. It ain't right."

Adeline looked down at her hand—at his man-sized hand holding tightly onto hers. She did not pull away. She closed her eyes. A battle warred in her heart. Withdraw or concede? Reason cautioned her to remain formal. Emotion encouraged her to welcome this informality, this closeness. She opened her eyes and examined his face intently. *Surely there is no harm in being his friend in front of the others. After all, everyone knows how close he be to Mr. William.*

Adeline finished dithering. With daring and determination she boldly declared, "All right, **Bill**. No more Mr. Isaacs."

"Good." Bill snatched the basket from Adeline's hand. "Now, let's go find some berries."

From that moment on, Bill Isaacs sought out every possible moment to be near Adeline. He always had a credible excuse to visit her. She needed more firewood for the

Strangers and Sojourners in a Town Called Penryn:

ADELINE

kitchen stove. The water pump needed fixin'. A raccoon nesting under the house needed to be extracted.

Lonesome for company, Adeline began to anticipate Bill's unexpected callings at the house. One Sunday, a week after they had openly declared their friendship, she cooked an extra portion for the noon-day dinner, *"jes' in case Bill be stoppin' by today."* He, indeed, just happened to be near the house and came in to say "hello" to his *friend*. He lingered after the Sunday dinner until it was time for the Sunday supper. He helped Adeline clear the table after each of the meals. He sat on a kitchen stool, watching Adeline wash and dry the dishes. He tried to help her with this chore after the noon dinner, but Adeline insisted on doing it herself. So, after the evening supper, he insisted on keeping her company while she tidied up the kitchen. The stories he told made her laugh out loud. Then, he started singing. Silly songs. Mining songs. Story songs. Church songs. The timbre of Bill's voice mesmerized Adeline. She stood at the dry sink, lost in thought, relishing the attention given to her by this amiable man.

Strangers and Sojourners in a Town Called Penryn:

ADELINE

"Adeline? Addie?" Bill's whisper, so close to her ear, brought Adeline's attention back to the present. She startled at how close he stood behind her, his warm breath circulating around the back of her neck. He whispered again. "Adeline, my dear. Are you alright?" He slowly wrapped his arms around her waist, drawing the still silent Adeline closer to himself. Gently, methodically, he kissed her neck. Adeline's breathing quickened. She closed her eyes. *This cain't be happenin'. How can he want me like this? I be nothing, nobody, a black woman.*

Yet, Adeline welcomed Bill's touch. She, at thirty-one years of age, longed for this intimacy. Most unmarried women her age yearned for a husband, a family, a home, no matter what race they may be. *Jes' 'cuz I be colored ain't mean I ain't wanting the same as ev'ryone else.*

Bill rested his chin on Adeline's shoulder, still holding her firmly against him.

Formality arose. "Mr. Isaacs. . .I ain't sure 'bout this."

Bill remained silent. He kissed Adeline's ear.

"Mr. Isaacs, please. I needs to think."

Strangers and Sojourners in a Town Called Penryn:

ADELINE

Silence. He kissed her once more on the nape of her neck then unhurriedly let go of Adeline. He stepped back a bit, waiting for her to turn around.

She placed her shaking hands on the sink and leaned forward, unsteady on her feet. Bill moved to support her but Adeline waved him away. He remained behind her, waiting.

Still facing away from Bill, Adeline spoke. "Are you funnin' with me, Mr. Issacs?"

No response.

"It be cruel to be funnin' about such things." Her voiced cracked on the word 'things'.

No response.

"Mr. Isaacs...Bill."

She finally turned to confront him. "Bill."

He spoke. "You are what I need, Adeline. Now, and forever."

Adeline inched closer to Bill. "You be sure, Bill?"

He inched closer to Adeline. Holding her face with his hands, he avowed, "I 'be' sure, Adeline. I be sure." He placed a tender kiss on Adeline's cheek. "I be sure."

Strangers and Sojourners in a Town Called Penryn:

ADELINE

"Bill! Time to wake up! Breakfast be ready in jes' a minute. Get yourself in here!"

"I think you need to come in here and wake me up!" His voice was groggy with sleep and longing.

"Oh, no, sir. I know your tricks!" Adeline smiled to herself. This scene had played out daily for the past three weeks. Adeline would protest. Bill would cajole. Adeline would give in. Bill would be satisfied. Adeline would be loved.

After breakfast, Bill would slip out the back door, saddle his horse, then ride away on the back trail of the property. The other workers would arrive shortly after Bill's departure. Then Bill would appear, traveling down the main road to the property, as if coming from the boarding house.

Adeline watched him depart. The daylight hours that they were apart were too long. Their night-time hours together, never long enough.

Strangers and Sojourners in a Town Called Penryn:

ADELINE

Chapter 28

*On my bed by night I sought him whom my soul loves;
I sought him, but found him not.
Song of Solomon 3:1*

The morning sun's rays filtered through the window and rested on Adeline's bed. Normally, the first of dawn's light would rouse her from her slumber, signaling the start of a new day. But Adeline had not slept last night, not a bit. Instead, she had sat at the dormer window, watching the night shadows. Waiting for the sunrise. She hadn't even bothered to change into her night clothes, knowing that sleep would not come. Ultimatums were to be issued—choices to be made. During this night vigil, Adeline had pondered her situation. Mr. William and Miz Rhoda had been home for nearly four weeks and Bill had yet to declare his intentions to William. After an entire month of waiting, of expecting, of believing, Adeline needed to confront her reluctant suitor.

She continued to watch the roadway. A small cloud of dust rose up from the line of oak trees that bordered the

Strangers and Sojourners in a Town Called Penryn:

ADELINE

roadway, signaling the arrival of the workers' foreman—of her Bill. Slowly, she got up from the rocking chair, picked up her shawl, wrapped it around her shoulders and quietly descended the staircase, careful to avoid the next-to-last squeaky step. As she made her way to the stables, Bill rode up behind her. Surprise registered on his face but Adeline could not discern if it was from pleasure or disdain.

"Mr. Isaacs."

"Adeline."

"Bill," her voice trembling, "Bill. It be time to talk to Mr. William."

"What am I going to talk to him about, Adeline?" His tone mocking.

"Well, you know'd, Bill, about, um, about us." She moved closer to him but he turned away, leading his horse to a stall.

"There is nothing to tell, Adeline. We had a bit of fun, enjoyed each other's company in bed, out of bed, in the orchard, and wherever you wanted. Shall I tell your precious Mr. William all about our many dalliances? How

Strangers and Sojourners in a Town Called Penryn:

ADELINE

would he feel then, about you, his black, unchaste, immoral, adopted daughter?"

Tears formed in her eyes but she willed them to not fall.

"Bill. You done tol' me you loved me; you wanted to be with me. I done give myself to you 'cuz of your wantin' **me!** You said you be my man. And you be knowin' that you be my first and only man for me."

"Ha! The only one? Do you think I am a dolt? Everyone knows what you and William been up to all these years."

"Taint so, Bill, taint so." Defiance crept into her voice, replacing deference. "You been my first and you be my last." Her tone hardened. All traces of despair gone. She raised her chin and looked him square in the eyes.

"When the baby be born, all will see you be the father, you with your irish-red hair and freckles. What then Mr. Isaacs?"

The announcement caught Bill off guard. He stammered a bit before declaring, "I will deny it to my dying day. Who will people believe? An outstanding member of

Strangers and Sojourners in a Town Called Penryn:

ADELINE

the community or old man Barton's colored whore?" With this last hurtful invective, Bill jumped back onto his horse and galloped away, leaving Adeline behind to deal with her growing dilemma on her own.

***

William sat at the table, letting his noon-day repast settle before going back to work in the orchard. His hand rested by his plate. His thumb rhythmically drummed the wooden top. Rhoda placed her hand over his to still his uneasiness.

"William, why not go into town and see if Bill is all right? There must be a good reason for his absence these last several days. At the same time, you can take Adeline along so she can buy what we need at the store."

Adeline, listening from the kitchen, tensed at Rhoda's suggestion. Her fragile emotions, heightened by her condition, overruled her sensibilities. *Might be I see Bill in town, tell him I understand, tell him all will be right, tell him no reason to be scared, tell him we can be a family.*

Strangers and Sojourners in a Town Called Penryn:

ADELINE

She undid her work apron, snatching her hat off of the wall peg as she entered the dining room.

"I over-heard you be going into town, Mr. William. I be needing to buy some goods at the mercantile. Might I go with?"

William nodded. "Might as well find out what Bill is up to. I will pull the wagon out back. Be ready in ten minutes." He picked up Rhoda's hand, kissed the palm, and gave her a hug. "Pray for patience for me, my dear. That I go easy on the missing Bill Isaacs."

***

Adeline waited for William outside of the store. Her packages of supplies stacked in neat piles at her feet. She scanned the streets for a sign of Bill. She watched the doorways of other businesses. *Where can he be?* Although the hurtfulness of Bill's last words to her still stung, Adeline worried for the man.

Bill was nowhere to be seen or found by Adeline. As William pulled the wagon to a stop, Adeline stooped down and gathered the packages and placed them in the back of the buckboard. William, uncharacteristically, re-

Strangers and Sojourners
in a Town Called Penryn:

ADELINE

mained seated. He usually helped Adeline into the wagon but today he remained stock-still as if bolted to the wagon seat. She managed to climb up unassisted and sat beside him. She noticed his fixed jaw, his pursed lips, his furrowed brow. Clenched fists held the reins. With his abrupt snap of the leather lash onto the horses' rumps, the wagon jerked forward. Adeline grasped the rail, the sudden jostling of the cart throwing her off-balance. William slapped the reins down again. The horses snorted, unaccustomed to such harsh treatment and broke into a gallop. With one hand, Adeline held onto the rail. With the other, she managed to keep her hat from flying off the top of her head. The hurtling wagon crested the hill within sight of Griffith's Quarry Works, yet Mr. William showed no signs of slowing down. Adeline let go of her hat. She wrestled the reins from William's grip and coaxed the now-exhausted horses to a gentle walk then stopped them completely. She turned to face William.

"What be wrong, Mr. William?"

William only stared straight ahead, shaking his head in disbelief.

Strangers and Sojourners in a Town Called Penryn:

ADELINE

"William?" Her voice barely a whisper. "Did you speak with Mr. Isaacs?"

He reached into his jacket and extracted a letter, smoothing out the lines and crinkles. Earlier, after he had first read the note, he had crumpled it in a fit of rage. Now, he stared at the paper, his hand shaking as he held it.

"Is it true, Adeline?" He carefully controlled his inner fury. "Mr. Isaacs left this note for me. He wrote that he had to leave town because you were going to falsely accuse him of fathering *your* child. Is this true?"

Adeline, empowered by a righteous wrath, answered calmly. "It would not be false to say so, Mr. William. Bill Isaacs be my soon-comin' child's father."

Seething, William recrumpled the letter then tore it in two, letting the pieces fall onto the wagon's floorboard. Exhausted from emotional turmoil, unable to speak, he peered straight ahead, waiting silently for Adeline's explanation.

"He courted me, Mr. William. Tol' me he loved me, no matter what other folks might think. Tol' me our being together was alright 'cuz he was gonna marry me. He

Strangers and Sojourners in a Town Called Penryn:

ADELINE

wanted me...and I... I wanted him. I wanted my own fam'ly. Is that so wrong?" She paused long enough to allow her words to penetrate William's wall of anger. When he did not speak, she continued.

"I be a thirty-one-year-old lonely woman who jes' wanted to be loved, Mr. William. The fault be all mine. I understand what you be feelin'. I understand why you be disappointed. First, your real daughter done deceive you then your 'dopted daughter go and do worse." Adeline rose and carefully climbed down out of the wagon.

"Think I take a walk, Mr William. You go on home, now. My walking will give you enough time to tell Miz Rhoda. Whatever you both decides about me, I accept."

Adeline walked dejectedly alongside the dusty road, found her wayward hat amidst the bushes, placed it squarely on her head, and then headed back towards home. The fate of her and her out-of-wedlock unborn child to be determined by William and Rhoda.

**Strangers and Sojourners
in a Town Called Penryn:**

ADELINE

Chapter 29

*But the Lord GOD helps me;
therefore I have not been disgraced;
therefore I have set my face like a flint,
and I know that I shall not be put to shame.
Isaiah 50:7*

Adeline lumbered about the house, hemmed in by the four walls. By mutual agreement and understanding between William, Rhoda, and herself, once Adeline started showing, her movements would be restricted to the house when the farm workers were about. As William had explained to her, ". . .so you will not be subject to ridicule by those who don't know the whole truth of your situation. Of course, you must prepare yourself for the scorn and contempt to come. Not only on yourself, but also on your child. People will be cruel, Addie. It is the very nature of man."

So as spring approached, Adeline's favorite time of the year, she was only able to view its daytime beauty from her bedroom window. When restlessness and melancholy overwhelmed her, she took to late evening strolls through

**Strangers and Sojourners
in a Town Called Penryn:**

ADELINE

the fragrant orchard. But instead of alleviating her despondency, the midnight meanderings seemed to only intensify her dark moods, the familiar surroundings bringing to her mind memories of her and Bill, strolling hand-in-hand through the trees, making plans for the future.

One of her memory verses came to mind—Catheraine's favorite verse. "Why art thou cast down, O my soul? and why art thou disquieted in me? hope thou in God: for I shall yet praise him for the help of his countenance." Psalm 42:5.

Penitent, Adeline knelt 'neath the flowering trees. "Jesus, I know'd I done wrong, but I still be trustin' in You. Now I be trustin' in You for my child as well." She lay prostate on the green field, allowing her tears to flow unchecked. Exhausted from her emotional turmoil and weighty burden of her unborn baby, she fell asleep. A nearby rooster's crow awakened her. The first light of the day shone though the flower-laden boughs alerting Adeline to the time. She arose and scanned the orchard, fearful that the workers had arrived and witnessed her predicament. Seeing that she was alone, she brushed the grass off of her skirt,

Strangers and Sojourners
in a Town Called Penryn:

ADELINE

smoothed her curls back into place, and hurried back to the house to prepare breakfast.

Rhoda and Adeline spent each evening preparing the layettes; one for Adeline's child, the other for Annelia's—both babies to be birthed at approximately the same time. This coincidence of pregnancies came in handy. No one questioned Rhoda when she purchased swaddling material at the mercantile, or skeins of yarn, or soft fleece.

While the women sewed and knitted, William reposed in his favorite rocking chair, listening to their banter. Adeline's condition had been a shock to him but more so to his barren wife. Rhoda's eventual acceptance of the situation came much later than William's. But, her acceptance was tinged with a bit of green—jealousy. Adeline heard Rhoda's little barbs but chose to ignore the remarks. Childlessness is a visible detail of a woman's private life, unspoken of in polite society. Adeline's compassion for Rhoda tempered her responses to the infertile woman's harsh comments.

Strangers and Sojourners in a Town Called Penryn:

ADELINE

"Have you chosen any *suitable* names, yet?" Rhoda's inflection begged the question of what would be a suitable name for a bastard child.

Unfazed by the inference, Adeline called out a few. "Peter, James, John, if'n it be a boy. Hannah, Sarah, Lucy, if'n it be a girl." Silence from Rhoda. The rhythmic click, click, click of her knitting needles the only rejoinder.

William salvaged the conversation. "All good, strong names, Addie. How about a middle name?"

"Well, Mr. William, I think one is enough. Unless you think two be better."

"No, I think one will do nicely. Easier to remember, easier to call to dinner." He chuckled at his own jest.

***

One June morning, during breakfast, William announced that he had business to do in Rocklyn and would be gone for a few days. He spoke with such authority that neither Rhoda nor Adeline dared ask for more information. Two days later, William returned. He gave no hint to what he had done while away. He brought back no supplies with

Strangers and Sojourners in a Town Called Penryn:

ADELINE

him. The perplexed women, baffled by his mysterious trip, gently pried for answers while eating dinner together.

"Did you have a nice trip, William?" Rhoda casually inquired of her husband.

"Yes, dear."

Rhoda tried again. "Were you able to visit with anyone that we know?"

"No, dear."

One more try. "Did you find what you were looking for, dear?"

"Yes, dear." He offered no further elaboration.

Stumped at his refusal to expound on the subject, Rhoda pouted. Adeline began to take up where Rhoda had failed but William put up his hand to her. "No use, Adeline. When the time is right, I will reveal the purpose of my trip. No more inquiries, please." The remainder of the dinner passed in silence.

Early Sunday morning, June 24, 1877, Annelia sent a messenger to summon William and Rhoda to the Lawson farm for the birth of her sixth child. The request did not in-

Strangers and Sojourners
in a Town Called Penryn:

ADELINE

clude Adeline. Even if Adeline had been invited, her present condition prevented her from attending.

Adeline gathered together the layette she had tenderly assembled for 'Lia's new baby and handed it over to Rhoda. "You tell Miz 'Lia that I be praying for an easy birthin'."

Rhoda patted her hand. "I will, Addie. And soon, William and I will be praying the same for you."

"Thank you, Miz Rhoda."

The couple returned home just before suppertime. Adeline, busy preparing the evening meal, didn't hear them enter. William forcefully hollered, "Hello, we're back!" to alert the preoccupied Addie.

Adeline started at the unexpected hailing. She came out to greet the two, wiping her hands on her apron as she came through the kitchen doorway. She raised her eyebrows at William, a silent questioning gesture.

"A girl. . .Eliza Catherine Lawson. Quite hale and hungry."

"And Missy 'Lia? She be fine?"

Strangers and Sojourners in a Town Called Penryn:

ADELINE

"Yes, she is already up and around, despite the doctor's advice to rest for at least a full day." William flung his hat on the table, mumbling louder that he intended. "Twenty-five-years old and six kids." He stomped off into the parlor.

"What be botherin' him?" Adeline directed her question to Rhoda who still stood in the back porch entryway.

Rhoda strode into the dining room, picked up William's hat and purposely placed it on the wall peg near the back door. She then pulled out a chair at the table and sat down. Propping her elbows on the table, she cradled her face in her hands, closed her eyes, and replied, "The doctor thinks that 'Lia is wearing herself out with childbearing. Wants her to take, ummm, precautions so as to allow her body to recuperate. Of course, head-strong Annelia just snorted at his suggestion."

"But she be alright?" A bit of fear crept into Adeline.

"Yes, Adeline. She is alright. She just needs to slow down a bit."

Strangers and Sojourners in a Town Called Penryn:

ADELINE

Adeline looked down at her belly, at its girth. *Iff'n I ain't be havin' this baby, I could've been help caring for her or the children, even though she be payin' no mind of me.*

Rhoda, as if reading her thoughts, reached out to her. "No need to worry, Addie. We both know that 'Lia is too stubborn and contrary to let the doctor be proven right."

Both women chuckled, knowing the truth of this last statement.

"Yes,m. She sure be both those things. Well, how's 'bout supper?" Adeline waddled out to the kitchen, her spirits much brighter.

Strangers and Sojourners in a Town Called Penryn:

ADELINE

Chapter 30

*Forget the former things; do not dwell on the past.
See, I am doing a new thing!
Now it springs up; do you not perceive it?
Isaiah 43:18-19*

Tap, tap, tap. Adeline, cat-napping upstairs, heard someone knocking quietly at the back door. She listened to see if Rhoda would receive the unanticipated guest. Tap, tap, tap...the knocking a bit more intentional. Still, no sound of Rhoda answering. When the caller began rapping again, Adeline hoisted herself up from her bed, the task leaving her panting for air. *This baby better be acomin' soon. Cain't take much more of this heaviness.*

She doddered down the stairwell and reached the door just as the insistent visitor started thumping the door for the fourth time.

Adeline opened the door at the same time as a hand came forcefully down to knock on the wooden slab. Instead of hitting the board, the hand met no resistance and propelled its owner, a small, stout, black woman, forward into

Strangers and Sojourners in a Town Called Penryn:

ADELINE

the dining room. Adeline caught the lady's arm and managed to keep her from falling headlong onto the floor. Exhausted by this effort, Adeline pulled out a chair and unceremoniously plopped down on it. She tried to speak, but her breathing was so labored that was only able to emit a wheezing gasp.

The mysterious intruder hurried over to Adeline, felt her forehead, and asked, "Where be the kitchen?" Adeline pointed to the room. The woman dashed into the other room, splashed some water from a pitcher unto a dish towel, then returned to Adeline. Placing the cold compress on Addie's head, the woman then took the patient's wrist, taking note of the pulse. "Tsk, tsk, tsk," was all she said to Adeline. She then took note of Adeline's swollen ankles. "Tsk, tsk, tsk." She scurried back into the kitchen, filled up the teakettle, and set it on the stove to heat. While waiting for the water to get warm, she filled a tall glass with fresh water and carried it out to the dining table, set it before the pregnant Adeline and commanded, "Drink." Adeline, unaccustomed to such bossiness, dutifully emptied the glass. The woman carried the now empty glass back to the

Strangers and Sojourners in a Town Called Penryn:

ADELINE

kitchen, filled it up again, and brought it back to Adeline with the same order, "Drink."

A screech from the teakettle called out to the ministering angel. The woman returned to the kitchen. Her rummaging through the drawers and cupboards created such a racket that Adeline raised herself up from table and hobbled to the kitchen entrance, astonished at such impudence from a stranger. She finally found her voice. "What you be looking for, Ma'am?"

"Epsom salts. You got any?"

"Yes'm. There be some under the dry sink."

The woman found the salts as well as a bucket stowed behind the sink and brought them both into the dining room, passing by the baffled Adeline in the process. She returned to the kitchen, fetched a pitcher of cold water as well as the teakettle and returned to the dining room, motioning for Adeline to follow and then ordered, "Sit."

The interloper dumped a cup of the salts into the tin bucket, poured the hot water over the crystals, swished the bucket around until they were completely absorbed into the water, tested the temperature of the mixture, poured in a bit

Strangers and Sojourners in a Town Called Penryn:

ADELINE

of cold water, tested the temperature again, then placed the bucket next to Adeline's feet. Bending down, she proceeded to gently remove Adeline's shoes and socks, carefully raised the pregnant woman's now bare feet, and lowered them into the warm water.

"Keep your feet in there until I says to take 'em out."

"Yes'm." Adeline dared not question this black Florence Nightingale.

Every now and again, the nurse retested the water's warmth, adding hot water when the solution had cooled.

"Ma'am," Adeline, at first hesitant to question the stranger, bolstered herself and plunged ahead, "Ma'am, I thank you for all your concern, but, jes' who you be?"

The woman snickered. "Why, Miz Adeline, Mr. Barton done hired me to help with your birthin'. Seein' the state you are in, we won't be awaitin' very long afore this baby joining' this world."

Incredulous, Adeline surveyed her. "You be a doctor?"

Strangers and Sojourners in a Town Called Penryn:

ADELINE

This time the woman snorted out loud. "Doctor? Good Lord, chile', no. I be the mid-wife. Mr. Barton came to me 'bout a month ago and made 'rangements for me to be here when your time comes."

At that moment, the door swung wide, thrusted open by William. "Miss Cora," he bellowed, "welcome to our home." Rhoda followed behind William. He continued, "I see you have met your patient. Let me introduce you all." Pulling Rhoda forward, "This is my wife, Rhoda."

"Pleased to meet you, Miz Rhoda." Cora offered her hand to the stunned Rhoda who mindlessly shook the woman's hand. When Rhoda finally found her voice she politely replied, "Miss Cora."

William commented. "I see that you have met Addie." Addressing Adeline, "Addie, this is Miss Cora, your mid-wife, and the objective of my trip a month ago to Rocklyn."

Adeline proffered her hand to Cora. The mid-wife reciprocated the gesture then instantly faced William, consternation in her voice. "Mr. Barton, this gal be needin' rest

Strangers and Sojourners in a Town Called Penryn:

ADELINE

until her time comes. Help me get her to bed so she can get off'n her feet."

Adeline, unaccustomed to such attention, dismissed the group. "No needs to be helpin' me up those stairs. I ain't dead."

Cora planted herself in front of Adeline. "Miz Adeline, we will gets along only if you don't be crossin' me. Now, we are gonna help you up them stairs and then I be takin' care of you for as long as you needs my help."

Shushed by Cora's authority and commands, Adeline meekly allowed the mid-wife and William to escort her to her bedroom. Cora helped Adeline undress from her everyday clothes then redress in a cool, cotton shift. She guided the worn-out mom-to-be to bed and helped her lay down on the soft mat.

The July heat permeated the attic space. Cora opened both gabled windows to their fullest, allowing a slight breeze to drift through the space, cooling the room by a degree or two.

Adeline, her energy spent, fell fast asleep. Cora tiptoed down the stairwell, trying to be as quiet as possible,

Strangers and Sojourners in a Town Called Penryn:

ADELINE

allowing her charge to replenish the strength she would need in bearing a child.

The birthing came the following Saturday, July 21, 1877. Rejuvenated by the care of the mid-wife, Adeline, with somewhat ease, delivered a good-sized, healthy, baby girl.

A beautiful girl. A mulatto—a mixed-race illegitimate child. The baby's coppery-brown wavy hair, olive-green eyes, and fawn-colored skin appeared incongruous to Adeline's coffee-brown kinky hair, coal-black eyes, and burnt-chocolate tinted skin.

People gonna talk. There be no question as to her being mixed. People will wanna know, be askin', "Who be the father?" Whisperin', snickerin', bein' holier-than-thou. Adeline cradled the suckling babe. *I will be protectin' you, little Lucy. So will Mr. William and Miss Rhoda. Together, we be makin' things right for you. Maybe you even be goin' to school one day, so you can learn to read and write. Jes' think, then you can read to your mama all them books that Mr. William and Miss Rhoda done read.* Adeline shifted

Strangers and Sojourners in a Town Called Penryn:

ADELINE

baby Lucy to her other breast. *Your life gonna be diff'rent. You ain't never gonna be a servant. Mama see to that. Yes, your Mama gonna see to that.*

The mid-wife rushed through the open door, dropping her shopping packages on the table. "Mr. William! Mr. William! All hell done broke loose!"

"Shush, Cora! Lucy be napping!" Adeline snapped at the distraught woman. Both women quieted, listening for the baby's cry. " 'Sides, you be forgetting that Mr. William and Miss Rhoda done up and gone to Sacramento for a few days?". Silence. Adeline drew Cora outside. "Now, what be wrong with you?"

"The town folks know, Addie. They be comin' up to me at the store askin' why I be at Mr. William's place. Somehows they found out that I be a mid-wife."

Adeline had prepared herself for this day. "Don't go afrettin', Cora. I know'd people were gonna' find out 'ventually. Might as well be sooner than later. When Mr. William be back, he will take care of the matter."

Strangers and Sojourners in a Town Called Penryn:

ADELINE

That same night, Adeline and Cora sat at the dining room table, enjoying a quiet supper. Drawn together by life's circumstances, they had become fast friends.

"Look at that sweet angel baby—a month old already. You be blest, Adeline."

A knock at the door interrupted Adeline's reply. She rose to allow the visitor in but her efforts were wasted as the caller entered on her own accord. Annelia flounced into the room, ignoring the two women. Spotting the cradle at the end of the table, her aloof countenance deflated. Her shoulders instantly sagged. "I. . .I. . .could not believe the rumors. . .I had to see for myself." She pulled the nearest chair to herself and sank down in it.

"Miz 'Lia," Adeline's began but her entreaty was cut short by the intruder.

"Please, Adeline," Annelia implored, "please tell me that this is not my . . .my sister."

Stunned, Adeline could only parrot, "Sister? Sister?"

"Yes. My *sister*." The last word hurled out of Annelia's mouth like an obscenity. She continued, ignoring the

Strangers and Sojourners in a Town Called Penryn:

ADELINE

looks of surprise and befuddlement on the black women's faces. "The latest gossip going round is that since Rhoda was unable to bear a child, she gave her permission for her husband, *my father*, to sire a child by you—you know, like the bible story when barren Sarah gave her husband Abraham permission to conceive a child with Hagar, the handmaiden."

Now completely dumbfounded and embarrassed, Adeline calmed down the high-strung visitor by her uncontrolled nervous laughter. She finally sputtered out, "Them towns people gots too much idle time on their hands."

"Oh, thank God. Thank God. Thank God." Annelia raised her prayer to the ceiling. Her next impolite question served only to satisfy her curiosity. "Well, then. Who is the father?"

Adeline squared off against Annelia. "It be no body's bizness but my own."

Cora tried to mediate between the two before tensions escalated. Annelia and Adeline both silenced her with icy stares.

Strangers and Sojourners in a Town Called Penryn:

ADELINE

"It be no body's bizness, Miss Annelia. 'Nough said."

"No, Adeline. Not enough said. It is my business when this scandal affects me and my household."

"How can it be that it be affectin' you, Mrs. Lawson." Adeline spat out Annelia's formal name like an invective. "You got a husband, a home, children born *after* you be married. You done ev'rything right. I be the one with a fatherless child, conceived without a preacher's blessing, birthed in secrecy. I be the one to be scorned, not you."

Before Annelia uttered a response, Adeline pressed on. "What do you 'spose I should do, Mrs. Lawson? Scurry away in the middle of the night with my child? Go somewheres so you cain't be offended by my mistake? So YOU can walk through town without being uncomfortable?" She gasped for air yet continued on. "You gots everything, 'Lia. My baby Lucy be all I got, no matter how she came to be. I won't be ahidin' her. I won't be 'shamed of her. I won't be denyin' her a better life on account of how you be discomfitted by my misdeeds."

Strangers and Sojourners in a Town Called Penryn:

ADELINE

A tiny cry drifted from the babe in the cradle, interrupting Adeline's tirade. She slapped the tabletop with the palms of her hands. "'Nough said." She reached over and drew Lucy from the cradle. The child nuzzled her mother, searching for food.

Annelia, reproached and chastened, remained seated, witnessing the tenderness Adeline showered on her beloved, illegitimate child. She brushed away unwilled tears of anger from her eyes, got to her feet, and headed for the back door. Pausing in the doorway for a minute, she whirled back around and lashed out at Adeline.

"I will never understand my father's affection for you, for his obsession in caring for you. I have genuinely tried to be amenable to his wishes regarding my comportment towards you, yet the more I concede the more he demands. I am sure that he will expect me to accept your, how shall I put it, your... *spawn* into my family. It is something I cannot and will not do. From now on, as long as you remain here, I will not visit this house. I will not acknowledge your existence. I will not speak of you or your out-of-

Strangers and Sojourners in a Town Called Penryn:

ADELINE

wedlock, mixed-race, fatherless off-spring." After her last proclamation, she fled the house.

    Adeline, distressed by 'Lia's tongue-lashing, drew baby Lucy closer to her breast, as if shielding the child from the brutally hurled words.

    Cora merely responded to the tirade with a, "Humph" and "good riddance."

Strangers and Sojourners in a Town Called Penryn:

ADELINE

Chapter 31

But as for me, my prayer is to you, O Lord.
At an acceptable time, O God,
in the abundance of your steadfast love
answer me in your saving faithfulness.
Psalm 69:13

William and Rhoda returned from Sacramento City the following day. Sitting at the table with Adeline, William bantered with her about the sights of the city, the multitude of new buildings that lined the streets, the flux of Chinese immigrants establishing businesses on the outskirts of the town.

"One day Rhoda and I will take you and Lucy with us. Maybe after the child's first birthday. Would you like that, Addie?"

Adeline, distracted by her thoughts of the preceding day, failed to hear the question.

William leaned in closer to Adeline and restated, "Addie, would you like to go to Sacramento sometime?"

Strangers and Sojourners in a Town Called Penryn:

ADELINE

This time, Adeline heard William speaking, but didn't catch the actual question.

"Uh, 'scuse me, Mr. William. I guess I be somewheres else in my thoughts."

William scrutinized Adeline's face. "Are you going to confide in me, Addie? I can assure you, after all that has happened, nothing you have to say will unnerve me. Now, out with it."

Adeline fidgeted with a string on her apron. She pulled it so hard that it finally gave way under the tugging. She pocketed the broken thread then glanced around the room, making sure that Rhoda and Cora were out of hearing range. Eventually, she found her voice and enough courage to pour her heart out to William.

"Mr. William, you know how much I love you for all your goodness and kindness you done gib me over all these many years."

William reached out and held her hand. "Go on, Addie. Tell me what you are thinking."

Adeline plunged ahead, a rush of words spilling out. "I thinks, Mr. William, that it be time for me to find my

Strangers and Sojourners in a Town Called Penryn:

ADELINE

own way, for me to start earning my keep in this world. I be thinkin' of findin' a place for me to work so's I can provide for me and Lucy—to ready me for the time that you and Miz Rhoda won't be here to watch out for me and my child."

William studied her face. Adeline met his gaze. "If'n it was up to me, Mr. William, I would never leave this place. You have giv'n me a home, a fam'ly, a hope in this here life. But, I gots to think of the future, Lucy's future. I gots to make a place for her."

William, still holding her hand, admonished her. "Adeline, you will do not such thing. I made a promise to Catheraine that I would look after you until I am no longer on this earth. I intend to keep my promise. As a matter of fact, I have already taken steps to insure that my oath will remain, even after I am gone. You must trust me in this matter."

Bowing her head, Adeline quietly answered, "Yes'm, Mr. William. I be trustin' you. And God bless you."

Strangers and Sojourners in a Town Called Penryn:

ADELINE

Cora prepared to return to her hometown. Adeline's farewells to her new-found friend, though sorrowful, were tinged with joy and a promise. "I be calling on you, Cora, whenever Mr. William needs me to visit Rocklyn for supplies."

"You better, Adeline. I gots to see how that young'un be growing." Hugs and kisses followed.

Cora added, "And you listen to Mr. William. He is a good man. Don't go afrettin' about the time ahead. God put you where you needs to be and God and your Mr. William will watch over you and Lucy." More hugs and kisses—then departure. Adeline watched the wagon carrying her friend away, till it crested the hill and rambled out of the new mother's sight.

**Strangers and Sojourners
in a Town Called Penryn:**

ADELINE

Chapter 32

*The LORD watches over the sojourners;
he upholds the widow and the fatherless.
Psalm 146:9*

July 1878

A party? For a baby? Mr. William done gone plum' crazy. Plain to see he loves her like his own, but a party for turnin' one-year-old? Crazy.

William had insisted on a celebration for Lucy's birthday. He had made arrangements for a day excursion to Sacramento, traveling to and fro on the train, no less. Adeline's excitement for the up-coming trip spilled over onto her everyday tasks. She daydreamed—and burnt the cake. She got lost in thought—and added sugar to the gravy instead of salt. She woolgathered—and charred the fried potatoes.

Rhoda shook her head in exasperation at Addie's preoccupations. "I will be thankful when this trip is over,

Strangers and Sojourners in a Town Called Penryn:

ADELINE

Addie. Your absentmindedness is driving me to distraction."

"Yes'm, Miz Rhoda. I be back to normal soon."

The big day! William, Rhoda, Adeline, and baby Lucy arrived at the train station one-half hour before departure. To Adeline's astonishment, 'Lia was also waiting at the station with her husband, Leonard. Annelia's comportment testified to her own astonishment as well.

"Annelia, Leonard!" William called out to them. The couple waved to William and joined him at the platform. 'Lia hugged William, then Rhoda. She barely acknowledged Adeline, nodding slightly in her direction. Adeline nodded back.

An uneasy exchange followed the initial greetings. "Miss 'Lia, you be lookin' well. I hope baby 'Liza is growin' big and strong."

The situation forced Annelia to respond with politeness. "Yes, Eliza is well, thank you."

Strangers and Sojourners in a Town Called Penryn:

ADELINE

Adeline, non-plussed, continued with deliberation, all-the-while trying to converse correctly. "I am pleased that you and Mr. Leonard be, umm, are joining us today."

"It was my Father's expressed request that we accompany him and Rhoda on this trip. I was unaware that others would be joining us." This last statement she spoke loudly, deliberately, directly, to her father. She pulled her attention away from Adeline and started a conversation with Rhoda.

A quizzical expression covered Adeline's face. *Mr. William know that Miz 'Lia and I ain't on speakin' terms. Why would he want us together, today, in public? Ain't makin' sense.*

Adeline could tell that Annelia harbored the same suspicions by the way she glanced at her Father—the same quizzical look on her face as Adeline's.

Mr. William be up to sumpt'in. I jes' pray he knows what he be doin'.

The day passed somewhat pleasantly. Decorum prevailed. William served as a tour guide, leading the group up

Strangers and Sojourners in a Town Called Penryn:

ADELINE

and down the cobbled streets, pointing out the boats on the river, describing their functions, the type of merchandise they carried, and their points of origin. They dined at a hotel establishment where all were welcomed, even Adeline and Lucy.

After the meal, William ushered the group down the wooden sidewalk, passed by themany mercantile stores, then stopped in front of a lawyer's office. He opened the door and signaled for the family to enter. A young clerk escorted them to a large conference room at the back of the building. After all were seated around the table, William rose.

"I trust that you all have enjoyed the day. I planned this outing some time ago in the hopes that it would spur some sort of reconciliation between myself and my beloved daughter, Annelia." William looked fixedly at 'Lia then continued.

"I had also hoped that you, 'Lia, would come to some sort of truce in regards to Adeline."

Strangers and Sojourners in a Town Called Penryn:

ADELINE

Both 'Lia and Adeline looked down at their hands, avoiding eye contact with one another, listening to William's supplications for peace.

He continued. "Annelia Elizabeth Barton Lawson—you will always be my daughter, my only child, my continual reminder of Catheraine. There is nothing that will separate my love from you. You have blessed me with grandchildren, a legacy that will endure long after I am gone. You endured your mother's death, our separation, and unwilled loneliness at such a young age, yet you have triumphed through tragedy. While you may not have understood the measures I took to care for you, please know that I loved you with an irrevocable love. I always have and I always will."

William changed focus. "Adeline—an eight-year-old orphaned house servant with no last name. You came to Catheraine and I in our time of need, enduring a journey that uprooted you from the only life you knew in Mississippi, replanting you in this foreign land called California. Along the way you cared for 'Lia, becoming her nanny, playmate, and surrogate mother. You tended to Catheraine

Strangers and Sojourners in a Town Called Penryn:

ADELINE

during her affliction with affection and kindness and maturity beyond your years. You invaded our hearts, captured our love, and would not let us go." Overcome with emotion, William pulled a handkerchief from his breast pocket and dabbed his eyes. This last action affected his silent audience to tears.

William continued on, despite his wavering voice. "'Lia, I must tell you that the bitterness that has crept into your relationship with Adeline wounds me to my very core."

Annelia, sighing deeply, faced her father—her stern countenance softening. "Go on, Father."

"The disparity between you and Adeline only seemed to worsen with time. You have so much in life, while Adeline has so little. Yet, you resent her for what little she has." Annelia, listened intently to the harsh-but-true words.

"Today, Annelia, my daughter, you will have the opportunity to free yourself from this bitterness that hardens your heart, to free your soul to love happily, joyfully, unconditionally. In doing so, you will also free Adeline to

Strangers and Sojourners in a Town Called Penryn:

ADELINE

live her life unhindered by fear of rejection by you, whom she has loved since the first day she laid eyes on you."

Annelia sat silent, eyes closed, lips pursed. Her internal struggle outwardly visible on her face. With eyes still shut she whispered, "Yes, Father. I will adhere to whatever you wish as long as it is pertinent."

Although his daughter's acquiescence came with a stipulation, William accepted this declaration as a truce between her and Adeline. He lowered his head onto the table. None spoke. Annelia rose and drew next to her father. She embraced the wearied man, her action infusing him with strength. He reached out to her and began to sob. Adeline joined Annelia in consoling him. The others remained seated, unsure of what to do.

Minutes passed. William, emotions now in check but still unable to speak, motioned for Annelia and Adeline to return to their seats. A tap-tap-tap at the conference room door alerted the family to the lawyer's entrance.

"Mr. Barton, are you ready for the documents?"

Strangers and Sojourners in a Town Called Penryn:

ADELINE

William surveyed the room, the faces of those he loved and unsteadily replied, "Yes. I believe we are all ready."

The rhythmic clackity-clack of the train's wheels on the rails lulled Adeline and little Lucy to a light sleep. In her dream state, Adeline relived the day. *Did Mr. William really sign those papers? Don't seem real, my full legal name now bein' Adeline Barton. No more bein' named by who used to own me. No Adeline Avans or Adeline Goldstan. That lawyer done swore that Adeline Barton be my rightful legal name from now until forever. A true part of the Barton fam'ly. Cain't nobody tell me that I ain't belongin' no mores. And I have my own home, too! Them documents say I can live in Mr. William's house forever, even after Mr. William and Miss Rhoda passes on. Cain't be real. Cain't be true.* Clackity-clack. Clackity-clack. *Thank you Jesus. It be true that "To every thing there is a season, and a time to every purpose under the heaven."*

The screeching of the brakes stirred Adeline. She clutched the sleeping child, so innocent, so untouched by

Strangers and Sojourners
in a Town Called Penryn:

ADELINE

the world's meanness. *Your life gonna be different, Lucy Barton.*

She picked up the babe, adjusted the coverlet over the child's head, and stepped off the train. *Time to go home, Lucy girl. To our forever home!*

Strangers and Sojourners in a Town Called Penryn:

ADELINE

Epilog

Penryn
May 1962

    The second hand on the wall clock couldn't move fast enough for me. I stared icily at the timepiece, willing it to move faster, counting down the minutes until this day would be over. I had suffered embarrassment, loneliness, and humiliation. Embarrassment from having to stand in front of the class, 23 pairs of eyes focused on my plain dress, my too short bangs, my bruised knobby knees, while the teacher introduced me as the "new girl". Loneliness as I joined seven other students at the lunchroom table and no one bothered to talk to me. Humiliation as the cafeteria food ingested at lunch decided to make a later appearance in the classroom in the form of projectile puke—the half-digested hurled concoction landing on the starched, ironed, white ruffled blouse of my teacher, Mrs. Barry. This was a day I would never forget, no matter how hard I tried to dismiss it.

Strangers and Sojourners in a Town Called Penryn:

ADELINE

"Drrrrringgg, drrrringgg, drrrringgg." *Finally.* Grabbing my books and homework, I made a beeline for the door. I spied my brother coming out of his classroom and made a move to join him. Just as I did so, three other boys his age came alongside him, laughing and joking with him as if they had known him for years. Dispirited by his good fortune in finding friends so quickly, I lagged behind his group, too shy to approach them.

I began walking home, following my brother but keeping my distance. One by one, his friends veered off on side roads, heading for their own homes. When they all had departed, I tried to catch up to my sibling, but he decided to run the rest of the way home. I guess he was excited to continue exploring his new surroundings. So, I shuffled along, alone.

Once I arrived at the crest of the hill, I saw him entering our long, red-dirt, cracked driveway. I plodded onward towards the same destination but with less enthusiasm. I seriously needed some granny time, but granny and gramps had not moved to Penryn with us. As I approached my road to home, the nearest neighbor to my house was out

Strangers and Sojourners in a Town Called Penryn:

ADELINE

in her yard, gardening. She shielded her eyes from the sun so as to get a good look at me. I did the same to her. I thought my granny was old, but my goodness, this woman could have been my granny's granny. I slowed my walk. Then stopped.

She initiated the conversation. "Hello, there, young'un."

"Hello, Ma'am." I kept a safe distance, not out of fear, but just because.

"You comin' home from school?"

"Yes'm."

"You got a name, girl?"

"Yes'm. My name's Monica."

"Monica. That's a right fine name."

"Thank you, Ma'am."

"Enough of this Ma'am talk. My name is Mrs. Fiorito."

I worked the name around a bit before I acknowledged her again. "Yes'm, Mrs. Fee-oh-*ree*-toe." She smiled at my pronunciation attempt.

"You almost got it right, young lady. No matter."

Strangers and Sojourners in a Town Called Penryn:

ADELINE

I mulled over Mrs. Fiorito's age and decided to ask as politely as I could, "Mrs. Fiorito, can I ask how old you are?"

She chuckled out loud. "Well, you can ask, but that don't mean I have to answer."

"I didn't mean to be rude, Ma'am, it's just that I was wondering if you know about this town—about how it came to be. There seems to be so many strange buildings, and rock walls, and orchards." This time the elderly lady laughed so hard and long that I began to worry that maybe she wasn't quite right in the head.

"Girlie," she motioned to me to come sit down beside her, "come on over here. Come on! I think I can tell you a bit about this old town." I plopped down near her but not too near.

Mrs. Fiorito giggled a little more, as if thinking about a joke. "I know a thing or two about this town, alright." She pointed towards a building behind her. "You see that house?"

Strangers and Sojourners in a Town Called Penryn:

ADELINE

I turned to view a timeworn, used-to-be white, clapboard structure. I nodded to her. Her eyes twinkled as she continued on.

"Well, Girlie, I was born in that very same house on July 21, 1877. I've lived there all my life—85 years next month, to be exact. Now you know how old I am." She smiled at me with her hazel eyes, her light brown skin wrinkling at the corners of her eyelids.

"I know lots of stories about this here town of Penryn. Learned most of 'em from my mama. So, I guess the best place to start would be to tell you my mama's story. Well, would you believe it? My mama came to California in 1853 when she was just a child like you. Her name was Adeline."

The End of Book I

**Strangers and Sojourners
in a Town Called Penryn:**

ADELINE

Adeline in her later years

(Photo taken by her daughter, Lucy)

Strangers and Sojourners in a Town Called Penryn:

ADELINE

Made in the USA
San Bernardino, CA
28 May 2019